"I'm not your mistress. You may think I'm bought and paid for. But I'm not."

She babbled to a stop. He was looking at her as if she'd taken leave of her senses. "You don't own me." She soldiered on regardless. "And I won't be treated as if you do."

He shrugged. "Right enough," he said, then pulled down his zipper. The crackle of the metal teeth unlocking drew her gaze down. "Move over. I've a mind to join you in the tub."

"I most certainly will—" But her indignant reply backed up in her throat as his trousers and boxers dropped to the floor and her eyes fixed on his groin. Unfortunately *that* hadn't gotten any less beautiful, any less magnificent, than the last time she'd seen it. Her whole body began to shake.

She gulped, her mouth bone-dry, and forced her eyes back to his face as he stepped into the tub. The sensual smile made it obvious he was very well aware of the effect his nakedness had on her.

He settled beside her, his big body making the water and her temperature rise. "Now, where were we?" he said.

She lay transfixed by her raging hormones as he reached behind him for the soap.

kept for his
Pleasure

She's his mistress on demand!

Whether seduction takes place in his king-size bed, a five-star hotel, his office or beachside penthouse, this fabulously wealthy, charismatic and sexy man knows how to keep a woman coming back for more! Commitment might not be high on his agenda—or even on it at all!

She's his mistress on demand—but when he wants her body *and* soul he will be demanding a whole lot more! Dare we say it…even marriage!

Don't miss any books in this exciting miniseries from Harlequin Presents®!

Heidi Rice
HOT-SHOT TYCOON, INDECENT PROPOSAL

kept for his
Pleasure

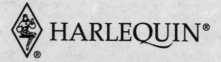

HARLEQUIN®

TORONTO • NEW YORK • LONDON
AMSTERDAM • PARIS • SYDNEY • HAMBURG
STOCKHOLM • ATHENS • TOKYO • MILAN • MADRID
PRAGUE • WARSAW • BUDAPEST • AUCKLAND

Recycling programs
for this product may
not exist in your area.

ISBN-13: 978-0-373-12857-0

HOT-SHOT TYCOON, INDECENT PROPOSAL

First North American Publication 2009.

Copyright © 2009 by Heidi Rice.

www.eHarlequin.com

Printed in U.S.A.

All about the author...
Heidi Rice

HEIDI RICE was born and bred and still lives
in London, England. She has two boys who love
to bicker, a wonderful husband who, luckily for
everyone, has loads of patience, and a supportive
and ever-growing British/French/Irish/American
family. As much as Heidi adores "the Big Smoke,"
she also loves America, and every two years or
so she and her best friend leave hubby and kids
behind and *Thelma and Louise* it across the
States for a couple of weeks (although they always
leave out the driving off a cliff bit). She's been
a film buff since her early teens, and a romance
junkie for almost as long. She indulged her first
love by being a film reviewer for ten years. Then,
two years ago, she decided to spice up her life
by writing romance. Discovering the fantastic
sisterhood of romance writers (both published
and unpublished) in Britain and America made
it a wild and wonderful journey to her first
Harlequin® novel, and she's looking forward to
many more to come.

To Bryony, for knowing when the
Elvis impersonator needs to be kicked out
of the manuscript.

With special thanks to Eilis, who made sure
Connor didn't sound like an extra from
The Quiet Man.

CHAPTER ONE

'YOU can't do this. What if you get caught? He could have you arrested.'

Daisy Dean paused in the process of scoping out her neighbour's ludicrously high garden wall and slanted her best friend, Juno, a long-suffering look.

'He won't catch me,' Daisy replied in the same hushed tones. 'I'm practically invisible with all this gear on.'

She looked down at the clothes she'd borrowed from her fellow tenants at the Bedsit Co-op next door. Goodness, she looked like Tinkerbell the Terminator decked out in fourteen-year-old Cal's sagging black Levi's, his tiny mother Jacie's navy blue polo neck and Juno's two-sizes-too-small bovver boots.

She'd never been this invisible in her entire life. The one thing Daisy had inherited from her reckless and irresponsible mother was Lily Dean's in-your-face dress sense. Daisy didn't do monotones—and she didn't believe in hiding her light under a bushel.

She frowned. Except when she was on a mission to find her landlady's missing cat.

'Stop worrying, Juno, and give me the beanie.' She held out her hand and stared back up at the wall, which seemed to have grown several feet since she'd last looked at it. 'You'll have to give me a boost.'

Juno groaned, slapping the black woollen cap into Daisy's

outstretched palm. 'This better not make me an accessory after the fact or something.' She bent over and looped her fingers together in a sling.

'Don't be silly.' Daisy shoved her curls under the cap and tugged it over her ears. 'It's not a crime. Not really.'

'Of course it's a crime.' Juno straightened from her crouch, her round, pretty face looking like the good fairy in a strop. 'It's called trespassing.'

'These are extenuating circumstances,' Daisy whispered as a picture of their landlady Mrs Valdermeyer's distraught face popped into her mind. 'Mr Pootles has been missing for well over a fortnight. And our antisocial new neighbour's the only one within a mile radius who hasn't had the decency to search his back garden.' She propped her hands on her hips. 'Mr Pootles could be starving to death and it's up to us to rescue him.'

'Maybe he looked and didn't find anything?' Juno said, her voice rising in desperation.

'I doubt that. Believe me, he's not the type to lose sleep over a missing cat.'

'How do you know? You've never even met the guy,' Juno murmured, wedging the tiniest slither of doubt into Daisy's crusading zeal.

'That's only because he's been avoiding us,' Daisy pointed out, the slither dissolving.

Their mysterious new neighbour had bought the double-fronted Georgian wreck three months ago, and had managed to gut it and rehab it in record time. But despite all Daisy's overtures since he'd moved in two weeks ago—the note she'd posted through his door and the message she'd relayed to his cleaning lady—he'd made no attempt to greet his neighbours at Mrs Valdermeyer's Bedsit Co-operative. Or join the search for the missing Mr Pootles.

In fact he'd been downright rude. When she'd dropped off a plate of her special home-made brownies the day before in a last ditch attempt to get his attention, he hadn't even returned the plate, let alone thanked her for them. Clearly the man was too rich and self-centred to have any time for the likes of them—or their problems.

And then there were his dark, striking good looks to be considered. 'All you have to do is look at him,' Daisy continued, 'to see he's a you-know-what-hole with a capital A.'

Okay, so she'd only caught glimpses of the guy as he was striding down his front steps towards the snazzy maroon gas-guzzler he kept parked out front. At least six feet two, leanly muscled and what she guessed most people would term ruggedly handsome, the guy was what she termed full of himself. Even from a distance he radiated enough testosterone to make a woman's ovaries stand up and take notice—and she was sure he knew it.

Not that Daisy's ovaries had taken any notice, of course. Well, not much anyway.

Luckily for Daisy, she was now completely immune to men like her new neighbour. Arrogant, self-absorbed charmers who thought of women as playthings. Men like Gary, who'd sidled into her life a year ago with his come-hither smile, his designer suits and his clever hands and sidled right back out again three months later taking a good portion of her pride and a tiny chunk of her heart with him.

Daisy had made a pact with herself then and there—that she'd never fall prey to some good-looking playboy again. What she needed was a nice regular guy. A man of substance and integrity, who would come to love her and respect her, who wanted the same things out of life she wanted and preferably didn't know the difference between a designer label and a supermarket own brand.

Juno gave an irritated huff, interrupting Daisy's moment of truth. 'I still don't understand why you haven't just asked the guy about that stupid cat.'

A pulse of heat pumped under Daisy's skin. 'I tried to

catch him the few times I spotted him, but he drives off so fast I would have had to be an Olympic sprinter.'

She'd suffer the tortures of hell before she'd admit the truth. That she'd been the tiniest bit intimidated by him, enough not to relish confronting him in person.

Juno sighed and bent down, linking her fingers together. 'Fine, but don't blame me if you get done for breaking and entering.'

'Stop panicking.' Daisy placed a foot in Juno's palms. 'I'm sure he's not even home. His Jeep's not parked out front. I checked.'

If she'd thought for a moment he might actually be in residence the butterflies waltzing about in her belly would have started pogoing like punk rockers. 'I'll be super-discreet. He'll never even know I was there.'

'There's one teeny-weeny problem with that scenario,' Juno said dryly. 'You don't do discreet, remember.'

'I can if I'm desperate,' Daisy replied. Or at least she'd do her best.

Ignoring Juno's derisive snort, Daisy reached up to climb the wall and felt the skintight polo neck rise up her midriff. She looked down to see a wide strip of white flesh reflecting in the streetlamp opposite and caught a glimpse of her red satin undies where the jeans sagged.

'Blast.' She dropped her arm and bounced down.

'What's the matter now?' Juno whispered.

'My tummy shows when I lift my arms.'

'So?'

Daisy frowned at her friend. 'So it totally ruins the camouflage effect.' She tapped her finger on her bottom lip. 'I know, I'll take off my bra.'

'What on earth for?' Juno snapped, getting more agitated by the second.

'The material's catching on the lace—it won't rise up as much.'

'But you can't,' Juno replied. 'You'll bounce.'

'It'll only be for a minute.' Daisy unclipped the bra and wriggled it out of one sleeve. She passed the much-loved concoction of satin, lace and underwiring to Juno.

Juno dangled it from her fingertips. 'What is this obsession you have with hooker underwear?'

'You're just jealous,' Daisy replied, turning back to the wall. Juno had always had a bit of a complex about her barely B-cups in Daisy's opinion.

She put her foot in Juno's sling and felt her breasts sway erotically under the confining fabric. Thank goodness no one would get close enough to spot her unfettered state. She'd always been proud to call herself a feminist, but she was way too well endowed to be one of the burn-your-bra variety.

'Right.' Daisy took a deep breath of the heavy, honey-suckle-flavoured air. 'I'm off.'

Grabbing hold of the top, she hauled herself up, her nipples tightening as she rubbed against the brick. Throwing her leg over, she straddled the wall with a soft grunt.

She peered through the leaves of a large chestnut tree and scanned the shadows of their neighbour's garden. Moonlight reflected off the windows at the back of the house. Daisy let out the breath she'd been holding. Phew, he definitely wasn't in.

'I still can't believe you're actually going to do this.' Juno scowled up at her from the shrubbery.

'We owe this to Mrs Valdermeyer—you know how much she adores that cat,' she whispered from her vantage position on the wall.

The truth was Daisy knew she owed her landlady much more than just a promise to find her cat.

When her mother, Lily, had announced she had found 'the one' again eight years ago, Daisy had opted to stay put. She'd been sixteen, alone in London and terrified and Mrs Valdermeyer had come to her rescue. Mrs Valdermeyer had given her a home, and a security she'd never known before—

which meant Daisy owed her landlady more than she could ever repay. And Daisy always paid her debts.

'And don't forget,' Daisy said urgently, warming to her subject, 'Mrs V could have sold the Co-op to developers a thousand times over and become a rich woman, but she hasn't. Because we're like family to her. And family stick together.'

At least Daisy had always felt they ought to. If she'd ever had brothers and sisters and a mum who was even halfway reliable she was sure that was how her own family would have been.

She looked back at the garden, gulped down the apprehension tightening her throat.

'I don't think Mrs Valdermeyer would expect you to get arrested,' Juno whispered in the darkness. 'And don't forget the scar on that guy's face. He doesn't look like the type who can take a joke.'

Daisy leaned forward, ready to slide down the other side of the wall. She stopped. Okay, maybe that scar was a bit of a worry. 'Do me a favour—if I don't come back in an hour, call the police.'

She could just make out Juno's muttered words as she edged herself down into the darkness.

'What for? So they can cart you off to jail?'

'Forget it, I'm not conjuring up a fiancée just to keep Melrose sweet.' Connor Brody tucked the phone into the crook of his shoulder and pulled the damp towel off his hips.

'He went ballistic after the dinner party,' Daniel Ellis, his business manager, replied, the panic in his voice clear all the way down the phone line from New York. 'I'm not joking, Con. He accused you of trying to seduce Mitzi. He's threatening to lose the deal.'

Connor grabbed the sweat pants folded over the back of the sofa and tugged them on one-handed, cursing the headache that had been brewing all day—and Mitzi Melrose, a woman he never wanted to see again in this lifetime.

'She stuck her foot in my crotch under the table, Dan, not the other way around,' Connor growled, annoyed all over again by Mitzi's less-than-subtle attempts at seduction.

Not that Connor minded women who took the initiative, but Eldridge Melrose's trophy wife had been coming on to him all evening and he'd made it pretty damn clear he wasn't interested. He didn't date married women, especially married women joined for better or worse to the billionaire property tycoon he was in the middle of a crucial deal with. Plus he'd never been attracted to women with more Botox and silicone in their body than common sense. But good old Mitzi had refused to take the hint and this was the result. A deal he'd been working on for months was in danger of going belly up through no fault of his.

'Come on, Con. If he backs out of the deal now we're back to square one.'

Connor walked across the darkened living room to the bar by the floor-to-ceiling windows, Danny's pleading whine not doing a damn thing for his headache. He rubbed his throbbing temple and splashed some whiskey into a shot glass. 'I'm not about to pretend to be engaged just to satisfy Melrose's delusions about his oversexed wife,' he rasped. 'Deal or no deal.'

Connor savoured the peaty scent of the expensive malt—so different from the smell of stale porter that had permeated his childhood—and slugged it back. The expensive liquor warmed his sore throat and reminded him how far he'd come. He'd once had to do things he wasn't proud of to survive, to get out. The stakes would have to be a lot higher than a simple business deal before he'd compromise his integrity like that again.

'Damn, Con, come off it.' Danny was still whining. 'You're blowing this way out of proportion. You must have a ton of women in your little black book who'd kill to spend two weeks at The Waldorf posing as your beloved. And I don't see it being any big hardship for you either.'

'I don't have a little black book.' Connor gave a gruff

chuckle. 'Danny, what era are you living in? And even if I did, there's not one of the women I've dated who wouldn't take the request the wrong way. You give a woman a diamond ring, she's going to get ideas no matter what you tell her.'

Hadn't he gone through the mother of all break-ups only two months ago because he'd believed Rachel when she'd said she wasn't looking for anything serious? Just good sex and a good time. He'd thought they were both on the same page only to discover Rachel was in a whole different book—a book with wedding bells and baby booties on the cover.

Connor shuddered, metal spikes stabbing at his temples. No way was he opening himself up to that horror show again.

'I can't believe you'd throw this deal away when the solution's so simple.'

Connor heard Danny's pained huff, and decided he'd had enough of the whole debate.

'Believe it.' He put the glass down on the bar, winced as the slight tap reverberated in his sore head. 'I'll see you the week after next. If Melrose is bound and determined to cut off his nose to spite me, so be it,' he finished on a rasping cough.

'Hey, are you okay, buddy? You sound kind of rough.'

'Just fine,' Connor said, his voice brittle with sarcasm. He'd caught some bug on the plane back from New York that morning and now there was this whole cluster screw-up with Melrose and his wife to handle.

'Why don't you take a few days off?' Danny said gently. 'You've been working your butt off for months. You're not Superman, you know.'

'You don't say,' Connor said wryly, resting his aching forehead against the cool glass of the balcony doors and staring into the garden below. 'I'll be all right once I've had a solid ten hours' sleep under my belt.' Which might have worked if he hadn't been wired with jet lag.

'I'll let you get to it,' Danny said, still sounding concerned. 'But think about taking a proper break. Haven't you just moved into that swanky new pad? Take a couple of days to relax and enjoy it.'

'Sure, I'll think about it,' he lied smoothly. 'See you round, Dan.'

He clicked off the handset and glanced round at the cavernous, sparsely furnished living room in the half light.

He'd bought the derelict Georgian house on a whim at auction and spent a small fortune refurbishing it, thanks to some idiot notion that at thirty-two he needed a more permanent base. Now the house was ready, it was everything he'd specified—open, airy, clean, modern, minimalist—but as soon as he'd moved in he'd felt trapped. It was a feeling he recognised only too well from his childhood. And he'd quickly accepted the truth, that permanence for him was always going to feel like a prison.

He turned back to the window. He reckoned a therapist would have a field day with that little nugget of information, but he had a simpler solution. He'd sell the house and move on. Make a nice healthy profit—and never be stupid enough to consider buying a place of his own again.

Some people needed roots, needed stability, needed for ever. He wasn't one of them. Hotels and rentals suited him fine. Brody Construction was all the legacy he wanted.

He dropped the handset on the sofa.

His shoulder muscles ached at the slight movement. Damn, he hadn't felt this sore since he was a lad and he'd woken up with the welts still fresh from dear old Da's belt. He squeezed his eyes shut. *Don't go there.*

Forcing the old bitterness away, he lifted his lids and spotted a flicker of movement in the garden below. He blinked and squinted, focussing on the shadowy wisp. Slowly but surely, the wisp morphed into a figure. A small figure clad suspiciously in black, which proceeded to crawl over one of the flowerbeds.

He jolted upright and braced his palm against the glass, his head screaming in protest as he strained to see. Then watched in astonishment as the intruder stood and dipped under one of the big showy shrubs by the back wall—a light strip of flesh flashing at its midriff.

'What the…?' The whisper scraped his throat raw as fury bubbled.

Damn it all to hell and back, could this day get any worse?

A surge of adrenaline masked his aching limbs and exploding head as he stalked across the living room and down the wide twin staircase. Whoever the little bastard was, and whatever they were about, they'd made a big mistake.

No one messed with Connor Brody.

For all the trappings of wealth and sophistication that surrounded him now, he'd grown up on Dublin's meanest streets and he knew how to fight dirty when he had to.

He might not want this place, but he wasn't about to let anyone else nick a piece of it.

CHAPTER TWO

'HERE, kitty, kitty. Come to Daisy. Nice kitty.' Daisy strained to keep her voice to a whisper as sweat pooled in her armpits and the coarse wool of the beanie cap made her head itch.

She scratched her crown, pulled the suffocating cap back over her ears and peered into the pitch dark under the hydrangea bush. Nothing.

Why hadn't she brought a torch? She huffed. And gave up. This was pointless. She'd almost broken her neck getting over the wall and had then spent ten long minutes searching the garden, gouging her thumb on one of the rose bushes in the process, and she still hadn't seen a blasted thing.

She crawled out from under the bush, her fingers sinking into the dirt as she tried to avoid squashing any of the plants in the flowerbed.

Raucous barking cut the still night air like a thunderclap. She clasped her hand to her throat and swallowed a shriek.

Her heartbeat kicked in again as she recognised the excited yips. Trust Mr Pettigrew's Jack Russell, Edgar, to give her a flipping heart attack—it had to be the most annoying dog on the planet.

She puffed out her cheeks and sucked on her sore thumb. Well, at least she could go back home now knowing she'd done her best to find the invisible Mr Pootles. Wherever he'd got to, it wasn't Mr Hot-Shot's back garden.

She stood, ready to walk back to the wall when the yapping cut off. The sound of a soft pad behind her had her glancing over her shoulder. She spotted the dark silhouette looming over her and had a split second to think. 'Oh, crap.'

A muscled forearm banded around her tummy and hauled her off her feet. Her breath whooshed out as her back connected with a solid wall of hot, naked male.

'Gotcha, you little terror,' muttered a deep voice.

She sucked in a quick breath ready to scream her lungs out, when a large hand slapped across her mouth—smothering her with the scent of sandalwood soap.

'No, you don't, lad,' the voice murmured, the hint of Irish in it only making it more terrifying. 'You're not calling your mates.'

She struggled against the band around her waist. It didn't budge.

Lifting her as if she weighed nothing at all, her captor hefted her back towards the house. The soap smell overwhelmed her as she listened to the grunts of her own muffled screams through the powertool now buzzing in her ears.

Daisy's head began to spin as tomorrow's tabloid headlines flashed across her mind. WOMAN SMOTHERED TO DEATH OVER MISSING CAT.

She kicked clumsily, connecting with thin air, and the baggy jeans slipped off her hips. Then the arm released and she landed hard on the ground, pitching head first onto the grass. As she scrambled up a hand grasped the waistband of her jeans and yanked.

'Hey, what's with the satin panties?' came the shocked shout from behind her.

She gasped, blood surging into her head as she lurched round and hauled the jeans back up to cover herself.

'Who the hell *are* you?' he yelled.

Silhouetted by the porch light, all she could make out of her captor were acres of bare chest, ominously black brows, waves of dark hair and impossibly broad shoulders.

Her whole body vibrated with fury as embarrassment exploded in her cheeks, but all that came out of her mouth was a pathetic yelp.

He reached forward and whipped the beanie cap off her head. She tried to grab for it but her hair cascaded down.

'You're a girl!'

She swiped her hair out of her eyes as outrage overwhelmed her. How dared he manhandle her and scare her half to death? She snatched the cap back. 'I'm not a girl,' she snapped, her voice returning at last. 'I'm a fully grown woman, you big bully.'

He took a step forward, towering over her. 'So what's a fully grown woman doing breaking into my house?'

She stumbled back, now holding the trousers in a death grip. Outrage gave way to common sense. What on earth was she doing arguing with the guy? He was twice her size and not in a very good mood if that threatening stance was any indication.

Forget standing her ground. Time to get the hell out of Dodge.

She turned to bolt. Too late—as strong fingers clamped on her arm.

'I don't think so, lady. I want some answers first.'

The forward momentum pulled her off her feet. 'Let me go,' she squeaked, tugging on her arm. His grip tightened as he dragged her backwards up the porch steps.

Panic welled up as he marched her through sliding glass doors into a massive open-plan kitchen. The smell of fresh varnish assaulted her nostrils and light blinded her as he snapped on a switch.

He hauled her past polished oak work surfaces and gleaming glass cabinets to a sunken seating area and shoved her, none too gently, into a leather armchair. 'Take a seat.'

She went to leap up but he grabbed the arms of the chair, caging her in. Heat radiated from his naked chest like a furnace, as did the heady scent of soap and man. She flinched at the fury in his face, which was now illuminated in every shockingly masculine detail.

A drop of water from his damp hair splashed onto her sweater. She shrank into the cool leather as the moisture sank into the fabric and touched her naked breasts.

Ice-blue eyes dipped to her chest and her traitorous nipples chose that precise moment to draw into excruciatingly hard points. Heat flared in her face. Why had she taken off her bra? Could he tell?

'Stay put,' he snarled, his laser-beam gaze lifting back to her face. 'Or, so help me, I'll give you the spanking you deserve.'

She began to shake, her heart wedged in her throat. Up close and rather too personal, the stark male beauty of his face was staggering. Dark slashing brows and angular cheekbones rough with stubble did nothing to detract from the cool, iridescent blue of his eyes, nor the livid white scar twitching against the tensed muscles of his jaw. As his gaze swept over her she noticed he had the longest eyelashes she'd ever seen.

They ought to have made those arctic eyes look girly. They didn't.

'You can't spank me,' she whispered, then wished she hadn't as his eyes darted back to hers.

'Don't tempt me,' he rasped.

Daisy's heartbeat sped up to warp speed. *Do not antagonise him, you silly cow.*

He straightened and raked a hand through his hair, pushing the thick black waves back from a high forehead. His gaze slipped to her chest again.

Her cheeks got several crucial shades hotter.

'You can stop shaking,' he said at last. 'You're in luck. I don't hurt women.'

The contempt in his voice was too much. Her temper flared, destroying the vow she'd made moments before. 'You just scared the crap out of me, Atilla. What the heck do you call that?'

'You were in my garden. Uninvited,' he sneered. Not sounding anywhere near as apologetic as he should. 'What did you expect, a red carpet?'

Before she could come up with a decent comeback, he turned and stalked over to the kitchen's central aisle. She noticed a curious hitch in his stride. Why was he walking as if he were on a swaying ship?

He bent over the double sink. Her eyes lifted to his back and she stifled a gasp, the question forgotten. A criss-cross of pale ridges stood out against the smooth brown skin of his shoulder blades. Daisy swallowed convulsively.

Whoever this guy was, he was not the rich, pampered, narcissistic playboy she'd assumed.

Coupled with the mark on his face, the scars on his back proved he'd lived a hard life, marred by violence. Daisy bit into her bottom lip, clasped her hands to stop them trembling and dismissed the little spurt of pity at the thought of how much those wounds must once have hurt.

Do not make him mad, again, Daisy. You don't know what he might be capable of.

He filled a glass with water, then turned back to her. Propping his butt against the counter, he crossed his bare feet at the ankles and stared. She shivered, suddenly freezing in the heat of the late-July evening.

He downed the water in three quick gulps. Daisy swallowed, realising her own throat was drier than the Gobi Desert. Probably the result of the extreme emotional trauma he'd put her through. She wasn't about to ask him for a glass, though. Keeping her mouth firmly shut at this juncture seemed like the smart choice.

He put the glass down on the counter. The sharp snap made her jump. He coughed, the sound harsh and hollow as it rumbled up his chest, and rubbed his forehead against his upper arm. Bracing his hands against the counter, he dropped his chin to his chest, gave a weary sigh.

Daisy let a breath out between her teeth. With those broad shoulders slumped he looked a little less threatening. When he didn't speak for a while, or look up, she wondered if he'd forgotten her. She eased out of the chair. The treacherous leather creaked, and his head snapped up.

'Sit the hell down,' he said, the huskiness of his voice doing nothing to disguise the snarl. 'We're not through.'

She sat down with a plop. He still looked enormous, and she suspected he was doing his level best to intimidate her, but she could see bruised smudges of fatigue under his eyes.

She ruthlessly quashed another little prickle of sympathy. Whatever was ailing him, he'd terrified her, threatened her and quite possibly let poor Mr Pootles die a long and painful death.

She'd be better off reserving her sympathy for the Big Bad Wolf.

'What exactly do you want?' she asked, pleased when her voice barely wavered.

He crossed his arms over his chest and cocked an eyebrow, saying nothing.

Completely of their own accord, her eyes zeroed in on the dark curls of hair on his chest, which tapered down a wash-board-lean six-pack and arrowed to a thin line beneath the drooping waistband of his sweat pants. The worn grey cotton hung so low on his hips, she could see the hollows defining his pelvis. One millimetre lower, and she'd be able to see a whole lot more.

The errant thought had Daisy's thigh muscles clenching.

Her gaze shot back up to find him watching her. The heat flared across her chest and up her neck. Did he know where her thoughts had just wandered?

He rocked back on his heels, still studying her in that dis-concerting way, and tightened his arms over his magnificent chest. Her heart gave an annoying kick as his biceps flexed, and her eyes flicked to a faded tattoo of the Celtic cross on his left arm.

She gulped, struggling to ignore the long liquid pull low in her belly. What was wrong with her? The guy might have the tanned, sculpted body of a top male model, but Daisy Dean did not get turned on by arrogant, self-righteous bullies, however buff they might be.

'So let's hear it,' he said, his soft, but oddly menacing tone cutting the oppressive silence at last. 'What were you about in my garden?'

She thrust her chin up, determined not to feel guilty. Her mission had been innocent enough, even if it now seemed somewhat suicidal. 'I was looking for my landlady's cat.'

He coughed, the dry rumble making her wince. 'How much of an idiot do you think I am?'

She bit back the pithy retort that wanted to pop out of her mouth.

'His name's Mr Pootles. He's a large ginger tom with a squinty eye,' she hurried on, despite the sceptical lift of his eyebrow. 'And he's been missing for two weeks.'

'And you couldn't come to the door and ask me if I'd seen him? Because why exactly?'

'I did, but you never answer your door,' she said, righteous indignation building. If he'd answered his damn door in the last two weeks she wouldn't be in this predicament. In fact, now she thought about it, this was all his fault.

'I've been out of the country this past week,' he shot back at her.

'Mr Pootles has been missing for two. And anyway I left messages with your housekeeper—and brownies,' she added.

His eyebrows shot up. Why had she mentioned the brownies? It made her sound like a stalker.

'Look, it doesn't matter.' She stood up, forcing what she hoped was a contrite look onto her face. 'I'm sorry I disturbed you. I didn't think you were in and I was worried about the cat. It could have been starving to death in your backyard.'

His eyes swept her figure again, making her pulse go

haywire. 'Which doesn't explain why you dressed up like a burglar to come look for it,' he said wryly.

'Well, I…' How did she explain that, without sounding as if she were indeed a lunatic? 'I really should be going.'

Please let me get out of here with at least a small shred of my dignity intact.

'The cat obviously isn't here and I need to get back…' She stumbled to a halt, edging her way round the chair.

'Not yet, you don't,' he said, but to her astonishment his lips quirked.

She blinked, not believing her eyes. Was that a smile?

'I got the brownies, by the way. They were tasty.' He rubbed his belly, his lips lifting some more. The smile became a definite smirk.

'Why didn't you answer my messages, then?' And what was so damn funny all of a sudden?

'They probably got lost in translation,' he said easily. 'My cleaner doesn't speak much English.'

He straightened, swayed violently and grabbed hold of the work surface.

'What's wrong?' Daisy stepped towards him. His face had drained of colour and looked worn and sallow in the harsh light.

He put a hand up, warding her off. 'Nothing,' he growled, all traces of amusement gone.

She could see he was lying. But decided not to call him on it. After the way she'd been treated he could be at death's door for all she cared.

He let go of the counter top, but didn't look all that steady. 'I know what happened to your cat.'

It was the last thing she'd expected him to say. 'You do?'

'Uh-huh, follow me.'

Gripping the edge of the centre aisle, he made his way across the kitchen. He moved with the fragile precision of someone in their eighties, his bare feet padding on the floor.

Daisy tramped down on her instinctive concern as she

followed him. She hated to see people suffering, and for all
his severe personality problems this guy was obviously suffering. But he'd made it clear he didn't want her sympathy,
or her help.

He shuffled to a small door in the far wall and opened it.
Leaning heavily on it, he beckoned her over with one finger.

As she stepped forward he pulled the door wide. She heard
the soft mewing sound and glanced down. Gasping, she
dropped to her knees. Nestled in an old blanket beneath a
state-of-the-art immersion heater was Mr Pootles—and his
four nursing kittens.

Make that Mrs Pootles.

'The cat showed up after I moved in.' She glanced up at the
husky voice, saw the hooded blue eyes watching her. 'She had
no collar and didn't want to be petted so I took her for a stray.'

Daisy studied the cat and her kittens. A saucer of milk had
been placed next to the blanket. She reached out a finger and
stroked one of the miniature bodies. The warm bundle of fluff
wiggled. Daisy sat back on her haunches.

Maybe the Big Bad Wolf wasn't as bad as he seemed.

A little of Daisy's anger and indignation drained away, to
be replaced by something that felt uncomfortably like shame.

'She had the kittens ten days back,' he continued, the
hoarse tone barely more than a whisper. 'The cleaner's been
looking after them. They seem to be doing okay.'

'I see,' she said quietly.

Daisy stood, resigned to eating the slice of humble pie
she'd so cleverly served herself by climbing over his garden
wall in the middle of the night.

Still, she took a few seconds to collect herself, brushing invisible fluff off Cal's jeans and then folding down the waistband so they'd stay up without her having to cling onto them.
Humble pie had always been hard for her to swallow. Having
delayed as long as possible, she cleared her throat and made
eye contact.

He was studying her, his expression inscrutable. She might have guessed he wasn't going to make this easy for her.

'I'm awfully sorry, Mr…?'

'Brody, Connor Brody,' he said, a penetrating look in those crystal eyes. Her pulse skidded.

'Mr Brody,' she murmured, her cheeks flaming. 'What I did was unforgivable. I hope there are no hard feelings.'

She held out her hand, but instead of taking it he glanced at it, then to her astonishment his lips curved in a lazy grin. The slow, sensuous smile softened the harsh lines of his face, making him look even more gorgeous—and even more arrogant—if that were possible.

Daisy held back a sigh as her heart rate kicked into overdrive.

How typical. When Daisy Dean made an idiot of herself, it couldn't be in front of an ordinary mortal. It had to be in front of someone who looked like a flipping movie star.

'So are your cat burgling days behind you, now?' he said at last, the roughened voice doing nothing to hide his amusement. He tilted his head to take in every inch of her attire, right down to Juno's Doc Martens. 'That'd be a shame, as the outfit suits you.'

She dropped her hand. Make that a movie star with a warped sense of humour.

'Enjoy it while you can,' she said dryly, trying hard to see the humour in the situation—which was clearly at her expense. She knew perfectly well she looked a complete fright.

'And what would your name be?' he asked.

'Daisy Dean.'

'It's been a pleasure, Daisy Dean,' he said, still smirking as if she were the funniest thing he'd ever seen.

'I'll come back tomorrow to get the cats, if that's okay?' she said stiffly, clinging to her last scrap of dignity.

'I'll be waiting,' he said. The hacking cough that followed wiped the smirk off his face, but only for a moment. 'I've a question, though, before you go.'

'What is it?' she asked warily, the teasing glint in his eyes irritating her.

Honestly, some men would flirt with a stone.

He didn't say anything straight away. Instead, his gaze roamed down to her chest and took its own sweet time making its way back to her face. 'Did you lose the bra on your way over the wall?'

Colour flared in her cheeks and her backbone snapped straight. That did it. 'I'm glad you find this so hilarious, Mr Brody.'

'You have no idea, Daisy,' he said, coughing out a laugh, his pure aquamarine eyes sparkling with mischief.

'I'm off,' she said through clenched teeth, not even trying to keep the frost out of her voice.

She might have been wrong about the cat, but she hadn't been wrong about him. He was an arrogant, overbearing, insufferable, full-of-himself—

A hissed expletive interrupted her cataloguing of his many character flaws.

She turned, watching in astonishment as he stumbled and then collapsed. The thud of his knees hitting the laminated floor made her wince.

She crouched beside him, her resentment fading fast as she took in his pallid complexion and the tremors racking his body. 'Mr Brody, are you okay?'

'Yes,' he hissed, a thin sheen of moisture popping out on his forehead.

She pressed the back of her hand to his brow, felt the scorching heat as he jerked back. 'You're burning up, Mr Brody.'

'Stop calling me that, for Christ's sake.' His head snapped up, the headache clear in his bloodshot eyes. 'The name's Connor.'

'Well, Connor, you've got yourself a very impressive fever. You need to see a doctor.'

'I'm okay,' he said, gripping the work surface. She offered

her hand, but he shrugged it off as he struggled onto his feet, the muscles in his arms bulging as he hauled himself upright.

She could see the effort had cost him as he stood with his hands braced on the polished wood. His chest heaved in ragged pants and the fine sheen of sweat turned to rivulets running down his temples.

'You can leave any time now.' He grunted without looking round.

She came to stand next to him, could feel the heat and resentment pulsing off him. 'What? When I'm having so much fun watching you suffer?'

The tremor became a shake. 'Get lost, will you?'

She rolled her eyeballs. Men! What exactly was so terrible about asking for help? Propping herself against his side, she put an arm round his waist. 'How far to your bedroom?'

'There's a spare room across the hall.' The words had the texture of sandpaper scraping over his throat. 'Which I can get to under my own steam.'

She doubted that, given the way he was leaning on her to stay upright. 'Don't be silly,' she said briskly. 'You can hardly walk.'

To her surprise, he didn't put up any more protests as she led him out of the kitchen and across a hallway. The spare room was as palatial as expected, with wide French doors leading out into the garden. She eased him down onto the large divan bed in the dim light, his skin now slick with sweat. He shivered violently, his teeth chattering as he spoke.

'Fine, now leave me be.'

He sounded so annoyed she smiled. The tables had certainly turned. She didn't have long to savour the moment though as brutal coughs rocked his chest.

'I'm calling the doctor.'

'It's only a cold.' The protest didn't sound convincing punctuated by the harsh coughing.

'More like pneumonia,' she said.

'No one gets pneumonia in July.' He tried to say something

else, but his shadowy form convulsed on the bed as he succumbed to another savage coughing fit.

She rushed back into the kitchen, spotted the phone on the far wall and pumped in the number for her local GP. Maya Patel lived two streets over and owed her a favour since the mother-and-baby club fund-raiser she'd helped organise a month ago. Her friend sounded sleepy when she picked up. Daisy rattled out her panicked plea and Connor's address.

'Fine,' Maya said wearily. 'You need to get his temperature down. Try dousing him with ice water, open the windows and take his clothes off. I'll be there as soon as I can,' she finished on a huge yawn and hung up.

Daisy returned to the bedroom armed with a bowl of ice water and a tea towel. The hideous coughing had stopped, but when she got closer to the bed she could feel the heat pumping off her patient. He'd sweated right through the track pants, which clung to his powerful thighs like a second skin.

She flipped the lamp on by the bed to find him watching her, the feverish light of delirium intensifying the blue of his irises.

'The doctor said to try and get the fever down,' she said.

She took his silent stare as consent and dipped the cloth in the water. She wrung it out and draped it over his torso. He moaned, the sinews of his arms and neck straining. She wiped the towel over his chest and down his abdomen. Her heart rate leaped as he sucked in a breath and the rigid muscles quivered under her fingertips.

The cloth came away warm to the touch.

'Dr Patel's on her way,' she said gently. 'Is there anyone you want me to call? Anyone you need here?'

He shook his head and whispered something. She couldn't hear him, so she leaned down to place her ear against his lips.

Hot breath feathered across her ear lobe and sent a shiver of awareness down her spine. 'There's no one I need, Daisy Dean,' he murmured, in a barely audible whisper. 'Not even you.'

She straightened, looked into his face and saw the vulnerability he was determined to hide.

He might not want to need her, but right now he did and Daisy had a rule about people in need—you had to do your best to help them, whether they wanted you to or not.

She rinsed the cloth, wrung it out and placed it on his forehead. He tensed against the chill, his big body shivering.

'That's a shame, tough guy,' she said as she stroked his brow. 'Because I'm afraid you're stuck with me until you're strong enough to throw me out.'

Connor closed his eyes, the blessed cool on his brow beating back the inferno that threatened to explode out of his ears. Every single muscle in his body throbbed in agony but those cool, efficient strokes, over his cheeks, across his chest, down his arms, doused the flames, if only for a short while.

He'd always hated it when his sisters had fussed over him as a kid, trying to tend the wounds their father had inflicted in one of his drunken rages. Even then he'd hated to be beholden to anyone. Hated to feel dependent. But as his eyes flickered open he was pathetically grateful to see his pretty little neighbour leaning over him. He stared at her, taking in the clear, almost translucent skin and the serene, capable look on her face as she soothed the brutal pain. She reminded him of the alabaster Madonna in St Patrick's Church, which had fascinated him as a boy, when he'd still believed prayers could be answered.

But then his Virgin bit into her full lower lip and shifted on the edge of the bed to dip the cloth back in the water bowl. His gaze dropped, taking in the enticing movement of her breasts and the outline of erect nipples against her skintight top. Despite the heat blurring his senses and the pain stabbing at his skull, Connor felt the rush of response in his loins.

He shifted uncomfortably and she turned towards him. Flame-red curls outlined her head like a halo and the vivid jade-green eyes grew larger in her gamine face.

She placed gentle fingers on his forehead, pushed back the hair that had fallen across his brow. 'Try to get some sleep, Mr Brody. The doctor will be here shortly.'

The desperate urge to take back what he'd said, to ask her not to leave, overwhelmed him. He opened his mouth to say the words, but nothing came out other than a guttural murmur. He grasped her wrist, grimacing as his shoulder cramped. He had to get her attention, make her stay, but however hard he tried he couldn't make a coherent sound.

'Don't talk, you'll only tire yourself out.' She took his hand in hers, folded her small fingers round his palm and squeezed. 'It's okay, I won't leave you,' she said, as if she'd read his mind.

He shut his eyes, let himself fall into the fiery oblivion, his mind clinging onto one last disturbing thought.

Would wanting to see his angel of mercy naked send him straight to hell?

CHAPTER THREE

DAISY placed Connor's hand carefully by his side, listened to the harsh pants of his breathing as he fell into a fitful sleep and then ran all three of Maya's instructions back through her mind—one of which she'd been pretending she hadn't heard.

She nipped over to the room's French doors, unlocked the latch and flung them wide. Maybe two out of three would do the trick. But the evening air was suffocatingly still, creating no respite from the heat.

Daisy sat back on the bed. She chewed her lip and concentrated on wiping the cloth over the contours of Brody's upper body. She applied the cooling linen to his arms and shoulders, and listened to the low groans as he struggled with the fever.

After five agonisingly long minutes, it was clear the fever had no intention of abating. If anything it seemed to be getting worse, the ice water now lukewarm in the bowl. Daisy wiped her own brow, cursing her smothering outfit for the umpteenth time that night.

Where was Maya? Shouldn't she have been here by now? But even as she registered the thought she knew it was a delaying tactic.

Brody shifted on the bed, his movements stiff and uncomfortable.

What was her problem? She should just take off Brody's sweat pants and be done with it. She was being ridiculous, behaving like a silly schoolgirl, when she was a mature, sensible and sexually confident woman.

Good grief, she'd seen naked men before. She'd lost her virginity at nineteen, to sweet, geeky Terry Mason. She wasn't exactly prolific when it came to partners and some of them had definitely been more memorable than others. But none of her relationships had been disastrous enough to give her a complex about nudity. Hers or anyone else's.

Until now.

Okay, Brody was a stranger, and his physique had affected her rather alarmingly already. But she could hardly let the poor bloke suffer because she'd had a sudden, inexplicable attack of modesty. And anyhow, this wasn't remotely sexual, she was only trying to get his temperature down until Maya arrived. Plus, he probably had underwear on. There was absolutely no need to worry.

That vain hope was crushed like a bug when Daisy peeked under his track pants and spotted the dark, springy wisps of hair.

She let go of the damp waistband so fast it snapped back into place. Brody moaned, sweat beading on his forehead in the lamplight.

Calm down, Daisy, stop being a ninny. You can do this. You have to.

She'd just ignore her pounding pulse and her quivering ovaries.

Right. She got up to look for some fresh linen, reasoning she'd need a sheet once she got the sweat pants off, to preserve his modesty. Not that she thought he had a great deal from his cheeky remark about her bra, but it seemed she had more than enough for both of them.

It took her approximately two seconds to find the brand-new bed linen in the dresser drawer. After spending a full minute undoing the packaging and snapping out the sheets, she was all out of time-wasting tactics.

Perching on the edge of the bed, she shook Brody's shoulder.
'I have to take your sweat pants off, Mr Brody. They're
soaked and we need to get the fever down.'

No response, just another hoarse groan. Fine, she wasn't
going to get his permission. She'd just have to hope he didn't
sue her when he woke up and found himself naked.

She hooked her fingers in the waistband, pressed her
thumbs into the damp fabric and sucked in a breath. She
turned her face away, heat pumping into her cheeks as she
eased the garment over his hips. Almost immediately, something halted its progress. She tugged harder, he grunted and
the fabric bounced over the impediment.

A few moments more of give, and then the sweat pants got
stuck again.

She fisted her hands and tried the same trick twice, but this
time the pants weren't budging. Anchored, she guessed, under
his bottom. She huffed, not ready to look round. Whatever that
bump had been a moment ago, she knew she'd got the pants
far enough down now to afford her more of an eyeful than was
good for her blood pressure.

She squeezed her eyes shut, gripping the band of elastic
harder, when he mumbled something and rolled towards her.
As the trousers loosened Daisy sent up a quick prayer of
thanks and gave them a swift yank. They slipped down before
he flopped onto his back again. She was leaning so close to
him now, she could feel the heat of his skin against the side
of her face, and smell the musky and oddly pleasant scent of
fresh male sweat and sandalwood soap.

Do not turn round. Do not turn round and look at him.

Daisy repeated the mantra in her head, staring at the open
doorway and trying not to picture long, hard flanks roped
with muscle as the silky hair on his thighs tickled the backs
of her fingers. She gave a huff of relief as she peeled the sweat
pants over his knees, inching along the edge of the bed as she
went. The effort to keep her balance and resist the urge to look

at him had sweat beading on her own brow. Concentrating hard, Daisy nearly toppled off the bed when her patient groaned again.

Daisy noticed the difference in sound immediately, her ears attuned to even the slightest change in tone. This groan didn't sound like the others, more a low, sensual moan than a painful grunt. Daisy puffed out a breath, damning her over-active imagination as her thigh muscles clenched and the sweet spot between them began to throb in earnest.

Get serious, woman. This situation is not erotic. Pretend you're undressing a sick child.

But however hard she tried, Daisy couldn't think of Brody as anything other than a man. A man in his prime. An extremely sexy, naked man who had something nestled between his thighs that had produced that resilient bounce.

As she was busy conjuring up some extremely inappropriate images to explain that damn bounce Daisy's luck ran out. The heavy, confining folds of the track pants locked around Brody's ankles. No matter how hard she tugged and pulled and yanked she couldn't unravel the sodden fabric and get the pants the rest of the way off.

Blast, it was no good, she'd have to look to sort out the tangle.

Keep your eyes down. Remember. Eyes on toes.

Muttering the new mantra, she swivelled her head and her eyes instantly snagged on something they shouldn't. Something that had her jaw dropping, her eyes widening and the liquid between her thighs turning to molten lava.

Wow!

She'd found the source of her bounce. And it was more erotic than anything she could have imagined on her own. Brody, it seemed, despite his fever, his delirium and his earlier exhaustion, was sort of turned on. His partial erection sat proud and long, angling towards his belly button.

Daisy swallowed past the rock lodged in her parched throat. She'd always been a firm believer that size didn't matter, but that was before she'd seen Connor Brody naked. Everything about the man was quite simply magnificent.

The sudden urge to run her fingertip along the ridge of swollen flesh was so all-consuming, Daisy had to fist her hands and force her gaze away. She stared at the ceiling and gritted her teeth. Utterly disgusted with herself.

How could she have admired his private parts like that? How could she have even considered touching them? How had she gone from frightened schoolgirl to raging nymphomaniac in the space of a few minutes?

What she'd almost done was unconscionable and unethical, a gross invasion of his privacy and against everything she'd ever believed about herself. She had absolutely no right to take advantage of the poor man when he was delirious and burning up with fever and needed her help.

She grabbed the sheet she'd laid out at the bottom of the bed and whisked it over him. It settled in a billowing wave over his lower half, but did nothing to disguise what was underneath. If anything, veiled in the expensive linen—the stark white standing out against his tanned skin—Connor Brody's naked body looked even more awe-inspiring.

She spent several seconds grappling with the sweat pants, finally freeing his feet, struggling to forget what she'd seen. But she couldn't.

Her eyes drifted back up and she noticed the small scar on his hip, which disappeared beneath the sheet. Her breath gushed out.

She'd always thought Gary had a beautiful body. Fit and perfectly proportioned, with that tantalising sprinkling of hair that had made her mouth water. Of course Gary had always thought he had a beautiful body too, which had taken the shine off a bit. But there was no getting round the fact that Gary compared to Brody was like Clark Kent compared to Superman.

Brody's long, lean limbs, toned muscles, the deep and, she now knew, all-over tan and that arresting face made quite a package all by themselves—not to mention his actual package, the memory of which was making Daisy feel as if she were the one with a fever—but even more tantalising was the hint of danger about him, of something not quite tame.

One thing was for sure, Gary naked had never had the physical effect on her Brody was having right this instant—and the man wasn't even conscious.

She couldn't catch her breath. Her skin felt tight and itchy and nothing short of a nuclear explosion had detonated at her core. And her ovaries weren't just quivering, they were doing the rock-a-hula—with full Elvis accompaniment.

Daisy frowned, contemplating what her unprecedented reaction to a naked Connor Brody might mean—none of the options being good—when the doorbell buzzed.

She leaped off the bed so fast she tripped on the carpet and almost fell flat on her face.

Brody must have heard her, because his eyelids flickered and he grunted before turning onto his side. Unfortunately, he took the sheet with him, flashing Daisy the most delicious rear end she'd ever set eyes on. She yanked the sheet back to cover his bare butt before her blood pressure shot straight through the roof.

Her heartbeat racing and her pulse pounding in her ears, she headed down the corridor to the front door. She took several deep breaths as she fumbled with the latch.

Get a hold of yourself. He's just a good-looking bloke and, from his rough, arrogant behaviour earlier, not a very nice one at that.

She tugged the door open to see her friend and local GP Maya Patel on the other side.

'This had better be good, Daze.' The harassed doctor marched past her with a loud huff, toting her black bag under her arm, her usually immaculate hair falling in disarray down the back of a two-piece track suit. 'I hope you realise I can't actually treat this guy as he's not registered with our practice. I could end up getting sued if any—'

She stopped in mid-sentence to gape at Daisy. 'Blimey, that's a new look for you. What are you? In mourning or something?'

Yes, for my nice, sensible, discerning libido, Daisy thought wryly.

'It's a long story,' she said as she led the way down the hall. The less Maya knew about the situation, the better.

'Who is this bloke anyway?' Maya asked, following Daisy into the darkened room.

'I told you, my new neighbour.' *And the harbinger of nymphomania.* 'I called round to ask about Mr Pootles and he collapsed in front of me.' *Sort of.*

'Let's take a look at him.' Maya sat on the edge of the bed, and plopped her bag on the floor. 'What's his name again?'

'Connor Brody.'

Maya touched his shoulder. 'Connor, I'm Dr Patel. I'm here to examine you.' She moved her hand to his brow when he failed to reply. 'He's certainly got quite a temperature,' she said, lifting her hand. 'How long has he been out?'

Daisy glanced at her watch, and realised he'd only collapsed about fifteen minutes ago, even though it felt like a lifetime. She relayed everything she knew to Maya, who began rummaging around in her bag.

'Would it be okay if I popped next door while you examine him?' Daisy asked. 'I'll be right back as soon as I tell Juno what's going on.'

'Sure, it shouldn't take long,' Maya replied, fishing a thermometer and a stethoscope out of the bag. 'Looks like this nasty twenty-four-hour flu bug that's been doing the rounds to me, but I'll check his vitals to make sure it's nothing more serious.'

Daisy high-tailed it out of the room. She did not want any more flashes of Connor Brody's anatomy just yet. She'd had enough already to keep her in lurid erotic fantasies for weeks.

'Have you completely lost your marbles?'

Daisy ignored Juno's pained shout as she walked past her

down the corridor to her bedsit, the towel wrapped tight around her freshly showered body. 'I've got to go back there. He's really ill. I can't leave him to fend for himself.'

'Why not? You don't know the first thing about him.' Juno followed her into her room and slumped down on the bed. Her brows lowered ominously. 'What if he gets violent?'

'Don't be melodramatic. I told you, that was a misunderstanding,' Daisy said, riffling through her wardrobe. Connor Brody getting violent was one of the few things she wasn't worried about. 'He looked after Mrs Valdermeyer's cat. I think I've misjudged him. He's not a bad guy.' *Well, not in that way.*

She pulled out her favourite dress, a simple bias-cut cotton sheaf printed with bright pink blossoms. 'Once the fever's broken and I'm sure he's okay, I'll leave.' She certainly didn't want to be around the guy when he had all his faculties back. Brody unconscious was quite devastating enough, thank you very much.

'But it's the middle of the night, he's a stranger and you'll be in the house alone with him,' Juno whined.

Daisy paused in the act of slipping on her hooker underwear. 'I'll be perfectly safe. Apart from anything else, he's unconscious.' She presented her back to Juno after tugging on her dress. 'Here, zip me up. I told Maya I'd be back straight away.'

Juno continued to grumble about personal safety as she zipped Daisy into her dress. Daisy tuned her friend out as she spritzed patchouli perfume on her wrists, put on her bangles and brushed the tangles out of her newly washed hair.

She knew why Juno was a pessimist, why she hid behind baggy dungarees and a scowl, and why she always saw the cloud instead of the silver lining. Juno had been hurt badly once, very badly. She didn't trust men. Which really was rather ironic, Daisy thought as she stared at herself in the mirror. After Daisy's grossly inappropriate behaviour in their neighbour's spare bedroom, Brody wasn't the one who couldn't be trusted.

'Why are you getting dolled up?'

Daisy stopped dead, her lip gloss in mid-air. 'What?' She met Juno's censorious gaze in the mirror.

'You're all dolled up. What's that about?'

'I am not,' Daisy replied, mortally offended. But as she focussed on her reflection she could see Juno had a point. The figure-flattering dress, the sparkle of bangles and beads, the signature scent of patchouli, not to mention the make-up she'd been applying, made it look as if she were planning a night on the town, not a night spent nursing a sick man. Shocked and a little dismayed, she shoved the lip gloss back in her make-up bag.

She most definitely was not dressing up for Brody's benefit; the very thought was ludicrous. She didn't even like the guy.

Daisy slipped on her battered Converse, forgoing the beaded Indian sandals she'd already pulled out of the closet. 'I'm not dressed up—this is me getting comfortable,' she said lamely.

She pretended she didn't hear Juno's grunted, 'Yeah, right,' as her best friend trailed after her.

'Don't wait up,' Daisy said, closing the door to her bedsit. 'I'm not sure when I'll be back.'

'Be careful,' Juno said, giving her one last considering look.

The crooked banisters of the old Georgian house creaked as Daisy made her way down the stairs. She noticed the peeling paint as she opened the front door, the patched plaster on the stoop. The house's imperfections had always made her feel comforted and secure. As she walked the few steps to Brody's door she couldn't help comparing Mrs Valdermeyer's cosy wreck of a house to the sleek, impersonal perfection of its neighbour.

Daisy sighed as she walked in.

The sight of Brody's naked body might have short-circuited her hormones, but she was not going to allow it to short-circuit her brain cells too. The very last thing she needed was for anything to happen between her and her arrogant new neighbour. He might be dishy, but she'd only needed to spend a few minutes in his company—and his home—to know he was so not right for her it wasn't even funny.

'He'll probably drift in and out until the temperature breaks,' Maya Patel announced, slinging her black bag under her arm. 'Keep dousing him with ice water. And if you can, get some more paracetamol down him in four hours' time.'

Daisy nodded, the butterflies having a ball in her stomach at the thought of the long night ahead.

'Are you sure it's not serious?' Daisy asked. Like most doctors, Maya didn't seem to think anything short of double pneumonia was worth getting excited about.

'I'm sure he'll be fine once he's sweated it out of his system. His temperature's hovering around one hundred and two, but that's to be expected. If it gets any higher give me a call. But his breathing's okay and he's a young, healthy guy.' Maya smiled at Daisy. 'Actually, if I wasn't here in a professional capacity, not to mention married and a mother of three children—I'd say he was a total hunk.'

Daisy dropped her head to concentrate on undoing the front door latch, her cheeks boiling.

'He's been in the wars a few times,' Maya continued. 'But he seems to have come through them surprisingly well.'

'You mean the scars on his back?' Daisy asked as she yanked the heavy door open.

'Yeah, do you know where he got them?'

'No, I hardly know the guy,' Daisy replied. Then her curiosity got the better of her. 'What's your professional opinion?'

'Old, probably from before he hit puberty would be my guess, but I'm no expert,' Maya said matter-of-factly, then chuckled as she stepped onto the stoop. 'And why, might I ask, do you care if you hardly know the guy?'

Daisy struggled to come up with an answer that wouldn't sound totally suspicious. She might as well not have bothered.

'Ah-ha.' Maya pointed an accusing finger at her. 'I thought so. Seems I'm not the only one who thinks our patient is a hunk.'

'He's okay,' Daisy replied flatly, praying her rosy cheeks weren't a total giveaway.

Maya jogged down the front steps. 'Let me know how he's doing tomorrow if the fever still hasn't broken.' She turned by the kerb and wiggled her eyebrows at Daisy. 'And keep an eye on your own temperature, Daze. Being in a room with a guy that hunky and that naked all night long can be hard work.' She winked. 'But I'm sure you're up to the job.'

She laughed as Daisy's cheeks shot from rosy to beetroot, and climbed into her car.

Daisy locked the front door and leaned back against it, focussing on the room down the hall where her hunk of a patient awaited.

A platoon of butterflies dive-bombed under her breastbone.

Hard work indeed. Maya didn't know the half of it.

CHAPTER FOUR

CONNOR awoke with a start to the dazzle of morning sunlight. The shadows from the long, traumatic night still lingered at the edges of his consciousness.

He squinted, threw his arm up to ward off the glare, and noticed several things at once. The hammer in his head had quit banging, his muscles had stopped throbbing in time with it and he was no longer sleeping in a sauna. He eased his arm down as his eyes adjusted to the light, gazed out at the leafy old chestnut in his back garden, and the last of the dark disappeared.

Hell, it was good not to feel as if he'd gone six rounds with the champ any more.

How long had he been out? He didn't have a clue. He caught a whiff of perfume: flowery, spicy and wildly erotic. Recollections from the night before washed over him: the pain, the heat, the terror. But more vivid was the recollection of calm words, of whispered reassurances, of firm hands soothing him back to oblivion when the cruel flashbacks had wrenched him to the surface. And all the good memories were wrapped in that enticing scent.

She'd stayed with him. Just as she'd promised.

He pushed up on his elbows as panic sprinted up his spine. *Where is she? Has she left?*

His heartbeat slowed when he spotted her curled up in the armchair across the room. He drank in the sight of her—like the icy water she'd made him sip through the night—then felt like a fool.

When had he turned into such a girl? The nightmares had stalked him on and off throughout his life, always catching him at a weak moment, but he'd learned to handle them a long time ago. They didn't bother him now the way they once had. It was good of her to stay last night, to see him through the fever and the familiar demons it had brought with it, but he didn't need her here.

But as he gazed at her a smile curved his lips. He might not need her, but she was still grand to look at in the daylight.

He folded his arms behind his head, relaxed into the pillows and indulged himself.

She'd changed her cat-burglar outfit, which was kind of a shame. The creased summer dress did amazing things for her figure, but the hint of satin at the plunging neckline, which he guessed matched her panties, meant her nipples were no longer clearly visible. Still, the pale, plump flesh of her cleavage was some compensation.

Her rich red hair, which had been springing out all over her head last night as if she'd had an electric shock, fell in soft unruly curls to her shoulder, framing high cheekbones. His lips quirked as his gaze wandered to her feet, which were folded under her bum, and he spotted a pair of battered blue basketball boots tied with lurid green laces.

The funky mix of styles suited her. From the little he could remember of last night, before he'd passed out, she'd been head-strong and prickly as hell—with a surprisingly soft centre when her angel-of-mercy tendencies had come charging to the rescue.

He sat up and swung his legs off the bed, glad that they didn't even wobble as he stood up. He wrapped the sheet around his waist, and his smile widened as he spotted his sweat pants neatly folded at the end of the bed. She must have stripped him. The smile became a grin. What he wouldn't give to have been conscious at that moment.

He stretched, yawned and rubbed his throat—pleased to discover the rawness gone—but kept his eyes on his angel of mercy.

Jesus, but she was pretty, in a cute, off-the-wall way. Not his usual type for sure, but then he considered himself very flexible where women were concerned.

Despite the horrors of the previous night, desire stirred. Then his stomach growled, interrupting the erotic direction of his thoughts—and reminding him all he'd eaten in the last twenty-four hours was her brownies.

The memory of the rich chocolate squares—crusty on the outside with a luxuriously moist centre—had his senses stirring again and his stomach giving another loud rumble of protest. She didn't move, her breasts rising and falling in steady rhythm. Connor's heart stuttered. She really had exhausted herself on his behalf. No one had ever done that before.

Once you factored in the gift of the brownies and her mad mission to save her landlady's cat, it occurred to Connor his sweet and captivating neighbour was quite the little Good Samaritan. Definitely not his type, then. But he still ought to thank her for being so neighbourly. At the very least he should show her there were no hard feelings for sneaking over his garden wall.

He chuckled. What he'd like to do was scoop her up and give her a long, leisurely kiss to show his appreciation. He resisted the urge. He doubted she'd thank him for the attention until he'd had a shower.

He strolled to the French doors, and closed the drapes. He'd let her sleep a while longer. Once he'd cleaned up and staved off starvation he'd wake her. He could offer her breakfast and then maybe they could get to that thank-you kiss if she wanted. No harm in seeing if they couldn't celebrate his recuperation together before she took the cat and its kittens and headed home. If he remembered correctly she hadn't been completely immune to him before he'd fallen on his face.

He began to whistle softly as he left the room. He felt a little shaky, probably from lack of food, but his other symptoms were as good as gone. It looked like another scorcher of a day outside, the morning sun making the garden's showy blooms look bright with promise. He'd call the French deli round the corner, get them to send over some fresh pastries and coffee and they could eat on the terrace. He fancied finding out a bit more about the intriguing Miss Daisy Dean before he sent her on her way.

All the stresses and strains of the last few days, the torments of the night, lifted as he bounded up the wide sweeping staircase to his bedroom suite. It felt good to be alive and back to his usual self. Anticipation lightened his steps, making him feel like a kid let loose from school on the first day of summer.

An hour later, Connor had indulged in a scalding hot shower, pulled on his favourite worn jeans and Boston Celtics T-shirt and stuffed down the last two brownies and a cup of steaming black coffee.

He peeked into the spare room and frowned. Angel Face hadn't moved. He padded into the room and squatted in front of her. Thick lashes rested on her pale cheeks and her breath scythed out in the gentlest of snores.

He caught a curl of hair that had fallen over her face, breathed in the spicy scent and then tucked it behind her ear. He skimmed his thumb over her cheek, felt the soft downy skin as smooth as a child's and fought the urge to kiss her awake. Still she didn't budge.

He cocked his head. Damn, but that position had to be uncomfortable, she'd have a crick in her neck when she came round and probably wouldn't thank him for it. She'd be better off sleeping in his bed. The sheets were fresh and she could lie down flat. It was the least he could do after all she'd done for him.

Never a man to second guess himself, Connor threaded one hand under her bum and the other beneath her shoulders and hefted her into his arms. She murmured something, then cuddled into his chest, her flyaway hair tickling the underside of his chin. Her scent drifted up and he breathed it in. She smelled delicious. So delicious he had a hard time controlling the rush of blood to his groin as he walked from the room.

She was surprisingly light, even in his weakened state it took him less than a minute to carry her up to his bedroom. As he placed her gently in the middle of the deluxe king-size bed it struck him how tiny she was. Probably no more than five feet two or three. Funny he hadn't noticed that the night before—no doubt the indignant scowl on her face had made her seem taller. He grinned again, his hands braced on his hips. He certainly hadn't managed to intimidate her much—and he'd been in a bad enough mood to give her a very tough time.

She stirred, squinting in her sleep. He strolled to the large floor-to-ceiling windows, where sunlight flooded the room, to close the curtains.

'Where am I?'

He turned at the soft murmur, to find his guest propped up on her elbows. She gazed at him out of those large mossy eyes, looking confused and wary—and good enough to eat.

'You were out cold,' he said as he finished closing the curtains. 'I figured you'd be better in bed.'

Her eyes popped wide. 'Mr Brody! What are you doing up?'

He sat on the edge of the bed, and smiled, touched by her concern. 'I'm right as rain, thanks to you.' He traced his thumb over the pulse in her throat, resting his fingers on her collarbone, and felt her shiver of response. 'And seeing as you've seen me naked, Daisy Dean, I think you best be calling me Connor, don't you?'

Colour flooded her cheeks, giving her pale skin a pretty

pink glow. He chuckled, desire stirring again, but a lot more forcefully this time. No, she wasn't immune to him at all.

What the hell? Why not let breakfast wait until after that thank-you kiss?

Daisy blinked, the last of the sleepy fog clearing from her brain. Goodness, those eyes, that face were even more devastating spotlighted by the shaft of daylight beaming through the curtains.

And his comment had brought back dangerous memories: of how delicious he'd looked naked—and just how thoroughly she'd assessed all his assets.

She pulled back, sat up. Did he know about that? Maybe he hadn't been as delirious as she'd thought.

'I'm so glad you're feeling better,' she said. She breathed in the scent of freshly washed male and was hit by another alarming jolt of memory. 'Sorry to pass out like that but it was a long night.'

'It was,' he said, the confidential curve of his lips doing very strange things to Daisy's heart rate.

'Right, well…' she edged back '…I should shoot off. You obviously don't need me here any more and I—'

He leaned over and grasped her upper arm, halting her retreat in mid-scramble.

'You'll not be running off,' he said, 'before I've a chance to thank you.' The mesmerising blue gaze dipped to her lips as the Irish in his voice became more pronounced. 'Properly.'

Heat flooded between her thighs. But instead of saying the polite denial her mind was screaming at him—something else entirely popped out of her mouth. 'How do you intend to do that?'

His eyes flared and he cradled her cheeks in his palms. His hands felt rough but unbearably erotic as he threaded his fingers through her hair, pushed the heavy mass back from her face. 'How about we start here?' he murmured, still smiling that devastating smile, his breath feathering her cheeks.

Then he slanted his lips across hers. The warm, wet heat was so shocking, and so unexpected, Daisy gasped. His tongue probed, firm and possessive, and her mind disengaged completely as the reckless thrill, the spike of adrenaline shimmered through her bloodstream.

He tasted of coffee and chocolate and danger. Forgetting everything but the feel of his lips on hers, Daisy sank shaking fingers into the silky black curls at his nape and drew him in as a drowning woman draws breath.

He didn't need any more encouragement. The kiss went from coaxing to demanding as he hauled her against him, his palm sweeping down her back. The weight of his long, strong body pressed her into the mattress as he pushed her down. She gave a staggered moan. This was madness, supreme folly and she couldn't summon the will to care.

As his lips stoked her into a frenzy she heard the hiss of her zipper. He reared back, breaking the kiss. Their eyes locked, his stormy with passion, the gleam of desire so intense she felt as if she'd been branded.

'You're beautiful, Daisy Dean,' he said, his thumbs stroking her nipples through the fabric as his eyes met hers. 'I want you naked.' The gruff statement was both question and demand.

She drew in ragged breaths, her arousal painful, as he tugged down the bodice of her dress, unsnapped the hook of her bra and bared her breasts.

She should have been shocked; she should have pushed him away. This was all wrong and she knew it. She'd been telling herself all night, she didn't even like this man—that he was not her kind of guy. But the time spent tending him, caressing fever-drenched flesh, hearing the broken cries of his nightmares, had formed a strong bond of intimacy that she couldn't seem to shake.

She'd looked into his soul last night, was looking into it now. They'd connected on some primal level and this was the only way to break the spell.

She wanted him naked too. She wanted him inside her.

His legs straddled hers and she looked down to see the ridge of his erection pressed against faded denim. Her fate was sealed as all her common sense dissolved to leave nothing but raw need clawing at her gut.

She shifted, but couldn't budge, pinned to the bed under him.

'You'll have to get off me if you want me naked,' she said.

'Good point.' His grin dazzled her. 'I'll race you,' he said, bounding off the bed.

She lurched into a sitting position, and watched mesmerised as he whipped his T-shirt over his head and his six-pack rippled. She looked away, determined not to be distracted from the task at hand by the muscular chest she'd spent most of the night memorising by touch. Anticipation surged through her. She was going to win this race.

She grappled with her shoelaces, cursing her choice of footwear. If only she'd stuck with the sandals. Finally she freed her feet, toed off the boots and flung them off the bed. She heard the thud as his jeans hit the floor, concentrated on wriggling her dress over her hips.

Heat blasted through every nerve ending as she looked up to see him standing before her, gloriously naked and his erection looking even more magnificent than she remembered it.

She bit into her bottom lip; her breath clogged her throat as excitement and trepidation seared her insides like a flashfire. He mounted the bed, grasped her ankle and gave a sharp tug. 'Come here,' he said, dragging her beneath him.

'Wait.' She braced her hand on his chest. 'I want to touch you.'

'Same here,' he said, cupping her chin. 'Let's negotiate.'

Then he kissed her, moulding their mouths together and crushing her body into the mattress. The coarse hair of his chest abraded swollen nipples. She dragged in a breath, let it shudder out as his lips trailed over her collarbone. His tongue slid fire across the swell of her breast and then his teeth nipped at the rigid peak and tugged. Rough hands kneaded her buttocks as his lips found hers again, the kiss so wildly erotic she thought she might be consumed by the flames.

She reached down, shaking with suppressed desire, and cupped his powerful erection in her palm. He shuddered as her fingers wrapped around the pulsing length.

She revelled in the feel of him, everything she'd imagined and more. His forehead touched hers, his whole body vibrating, his breathing harsh as she stroked and caressed him, learning the shape and texture as she had yearned to do all through the night. Velvet over steel. So solid, so warm, so responsive to her touch.

She ran her thumb over the thick head, felt the tantalising bead of moisture. He cursed softly and grasped her wrist, jerking back.

'You'll have to stop, or this'll be over before it's begun,' he rasped.

'I don't want to stop,' she cried, desperation edging the words. *Don't make me stop. Don't make me think,* her mind screamed.

I don't want to think, I just want to feel.

'Are you sure?' he asked. 'I don't want to rush you.'

She'd never been more sure of anything in her life.

'I want to rush. I'm ready,' she said, alarmed, need overwhelming her. She had to do it now, before the delicious fog of sensation cleared.

'Let's see how ready, then,' he murmured.

Before she could figure out what he meant, his fingers delved into the curls at her sex. She shuddered as he circled her clitoris and probed. She cried, gripped his shoulders, slick juices flooding out as she bucked against those knowing fingers, primed to explode.

He chuckled. The sound deep, husky and self-satisfied. 'Hell, you're incredible.' His fingers pushed inside her, his thumb grazing the hard nub. She moaned, clinging to the edge of control. 'But you're a bit tight, Angel Face,' he said, sounding regretful.

'What?' The question shuddered out on a breath of need— and confusion. Why was he still waiting?

He groaned, holding her buttocks as he pressed his erection against the slick folds of her sex. 'I don't want to hurt you.'

'You won't,' she gasped. 'I want you inside me.' How much more encouragement did he need? 'Now.'

'You're sure?' he asked again, making her want to scream.

She nodded, lifting her knees, angling her hips to accommodate him, so frantic she'd lost the power of speech. If he didn't get on with it, she'd die of need.

She was about to tell him so when he stilled, cursed under his breath and then, to her complete astonishment, pulled away from her and climbed off the bed.

She bounced up on her elbows. Horrified.

'Where are you going?' she cried out on a thin wail of exasperation. Had he lost his mind?

He bent to get something out of his bedside table. 'What's the hurry, angel?' he murmured.

Her eyes drifted down to that perfect rear end. Lust and frustration surged through her. She wanted to scream the house down. He'd worked her up to the point of meltdown and now he'd decided to rearrange his dresser!

'What's the hurry? Are you joking?' she squeaked, embarrassed by the desperate quiver in her voice.

He turned back gripping a telltale foil packet between his fingers and heat flooded into her cheeks. Even in her rampaging nymphomania, how could she have forgotten about protection?

'No joke,' he said, sounding ever so slightly smug. 'We wouldn't want any surprises.'

He knelt back on the bed, grinning at her as he ripped open the packet with his teeth and rolled the condom on. He put his hands over her shoulders, forcing her back on the bed, caging her in.

'Hasn't anyone ever told you, patience is a virtue, angel?' His eyes dipped to her tightly peaked nipples. 'Although, it should be said, there's not a lot of virtue in what I'm thinking right at the minute.'

Daisy's caustic reply caught in her throat as his lips covered hers. She rose up to kiss him back, letting the need, the sensation take over. But as she wrapped her arms round him, her fingers found the ridges on his back and tenderness welled up right beside the need.

His fingers gripped her hips and in one smooth move, he thrust inside her.

She sobbed, the fullness shocking her, the fury of sensations making her cry out. Then he began to move. Slow, heavy, insistent strokes that had the orgasm coiling ruthlessly inside her.

A staggered moan wrenched from her throat as the intense pleasure sent shock waves rocketing up from her core. She anchored her legs round his waist, sweat slicking her skin as she moved to meet each of his deep thrusts with thrusts of her own, and he drove deeper still. Her high-pitched pants matched his harsh grunts. Everything clamped down, her whole body glowing and pulsating as it rode the crest of a magnificent wave. The broken sobs echoed in her head as she burst free and exploded over the top—and heard his muffled shout as he crashed over behind her.

'That was amazing. You're amazing,' Connor murmured, stroking Daisy's cheek, then winced at the cliché.

But what else was he to say? Hell, if he hadn't been horizontal already he would have fallen over. He'd never had a stronger, more satisfying orgasm in his life. The experience had been literally mind-altering.

Using every last ounce of his strength he braced his arms

to stop himself from collapsing on top of the woman responsible and crushing her. Her eyelids fluttered open as he stared down at her. He grinned as she focussed on his face. She looked as shattered as him, those round expressive eyes wide with amazement.

Then her vaginal muscles squeezed around him in the final throes of her orgasm.

'God, sorry,' she whispered as the pink in her cheeks darkened to maroon.

She looked horrified.

He had no clue what the problem was—but with her still wrapped tight around him he was finding it hard to give a damn. Feeling the blood rushing back to his groin, he did the decent thing—with not a small amount of regret—and lifted off her. The next round would have to wait. Something had spooked her—and he didn't want to scare her off.

Propping his elbow beside her head, he leaned over her. His gaze swept her lush little figure and came to rest on her face. The flush of afterglow warmed her skin and dilated her pupils, darkening the deep green of her eyes, while the sprinkle of freckles across her nose defined those impossibly high cheekbones. She really was gorgeous.

She coloured even more, then looked away and tried to scoot out from under him. He locked his arm round her waist. 'Now where would you be going? We're not half finished yet.'

She wiggled, he held firm. Finally she looked at him, her cheeks now a deep and very becoming shade of scarlet. 'There's no time for anything else. I really have to be going, Mr Brody.'

His eyebrows shot up at the formal address. Then he simply couldn't stop himself. He threw back his head and roared with laughter.

When he finally got his amusement under control, she'd stiffened like a board, her bottom lip puffed up in a defiant pout as she glared at him.

He grinned. What *was* she about?

Women! He gave his head a rueful shake. They really were a whole different species. But didn't that make them all the more fascinating?

'Angel Face,' he murmured, loving the way her eyes narrowed, 'as we've just made love like a couple of rabbits, I think you'd best be calling me Connor.'

CHAPTER FIVE

DAISY was utterly mortified. But she couldn't decide if she was more annoyed by her own behaviour or the patronising look on Connor Brody's face as he held her trapped by his side.

'I don't feel comfortable calling you by your given name,' she blurted out. And then realised how prim and ridiculous it sounded.

Thank goodness he didn't bust a gut laughing at her again. But the twinkle in his eye made it clear it was a struggle not to.

'Should I make you more comfortable, then?' He pulled the sheet over her, flattening his open palm on the expensive linen and lifting his eyebrow as if willing her to share the joke.

Daisy felt the warm weight of his hand on her belly and turned away, feeling so exposed she wanted to die on the spot.

When she'd surfaced a moment ago to find him gazing at her, his face flushed, those sexy blue eyes intent on hers and his erection still gloriously firm inside her, the hideous truth had dawned on her.

She'd ravished a complete stranger. Had as good as begged him to make love to her.

Which meant she was her mother's daughter after all. Her mother, who had spent her whole life latching on to any guy who could give her a decent orgasm.

Daisy didn't know the first thing about Connor Brody. And he knew nothing about her. For all he knew she could be the sort of woman who made rabbit-love every chance she got. He couldn't possibly know she'd never ravished anyone before in her life.

The fact that the orgasm they'd shared had been the most incredible she'd ever had only made the situation that much worse.

When the muscles of her sex had clenched in response to the feel of him inside her, she'd been mortally embarrassed. Knowing she'd been tricked by her pheromones into believing they shared an intimacy, a connection, that they actually didn't.

Whatever way you looked at it, she'd used this man and his mouth-watering body to slake a temporary physical thirst—and fallen victim to her own libido. In so doing she'd broken the solemn promise she'd made to herself as a teenager, that she would never be like her mother. That she would never let her libido rule her life.

A calloused thumb skimmed down her cheek. 'What's the problem? Tell me and we'll see to it.'

Daisy swung round to face him. The tenderness in his eyes surprised her, but the lazy, confident, let's-humour-her smile on his lips contradicted it rather comprehensively.

Daisy felt her misery being replaced by irritation.

It really was a bit much of him to find the biggest identity crisis of her life so hilarious.

She sat up abruptly. She had to stop wallowing. Letting a total stranger witness her having a breakdown was not going to help matters. 'I'm absolutely fine,' she said, her voice as matter-of-fact as she could manage.

She grasped the sheet to her breasts, pushed her hair behind her ears, and felt a tiny bit better. She'd always been a woman of action. Once she saw a problem she set about fixing it. She'd have more than enough time later to analyse her wanton, irresponsible behaviour and what it all meant. Right now she needed to get the heck away from her studly neighbour before anything else happened.

The way he'd been studying her—all that smouldering

intent in his gaze—suggested he was planning a repeat performance. And she wasn't entirely sure she could trust her body not to take him up on his offer. Given what this little liaison had already cost her, another frenzied encounter with Mr Sex-On-A-Stick was the very last thing she needed.

'This is a little awkward,' she said. 'But could you pass me my dress? I need to be off.'

He made no move to get her dress, so she scooted down the bed, intending to lean over him and get it herself.

But as she did so he stroked a hand down her hair. 'What's the rush?' he murmured, his voice husky but firm. 'Let's talk about it. Whatever it is, we can fix it.'

She gaped at him over her shoulder. Would you credit it? The only time in her life she'd rather gnaw off her own tongue than talk about her feelings and she'd found the one man on the planet willing to share and discuss.

'Mr Bro…' She paused when his eyebrow lifted again. 'Connor, we had sex. It was great sex. So thank you. But I don't think there's anything else to say.'

Both his eyebrows lifted at that one. Clearly, her no-nonsense approach had shocked him but she soldiered on. 'We have absolutely nothing in common,' she continued, slipping off the bed. 'We're obviously totally wrong for each other.' She dropped her end of the sheet and whipped on her dress. 'This was strictly a one-shot deal after a difficult night.'

They both knew the score here, and if he thought they were going to have another quickie for old times' sake he could forget it—the first one had been quite devastating enough to her peace of mind.

She pulled on her knickers, scouted around for her bra, grabbed it off the floor and shoved it into the pocket of her dress. 'So why don't we call it quits and leave it at that?'

She straightened, holding one baseball boot as she scoured the luxurious deep-pile carpet for the other.

'Are you serious?' he asked. He hadn't moved, the sheet resting tantalisingly low on his hips as he stared at her.

'Absolutely,' she said, forcing a smile.

Noticing the way the thin wisps of black hair curled around his belly button, she swallowed and averted her eyes. To her immense relief she spotted the other boot peeking out from under the bed. She grabbed it and stood up.

He'd propped himself up on the pillows, and was still studying her, looking stunned.

No doubt with those dark, dangerous good looks and the masterful way he made love, having the woman do a runner was a new experience for him. Daisy couldn't muster much sympathy. He'd have to learn to deal with it. She had her own problems.

He slid his feet to the floor, the sheet now barely covering him.

Daisy threw up her hand to stop him going any further. 'Please don't get up. I can see myself out,' she squeaked. The last thing she needed was another full-frontal view of that mouth-watering physique.

Before he could say another word, she dashed out the door, barefoot.

Connor gaped at the open bedroom door and listened to the pit-pat of Daisy's footsteps as she hightailed it down the stairs.

The muffled slam of the front door echoed at the bottom of the house.

He flopped back on the bed, stared at the ceiling and frowned at the fancy light fixture his interior designer had insisted on shipping in from Barcelona.

What the hell had that been about?

He might as well have set her tail on fire, she'd shot out of the room so fast. Either he'd been hallucinating, or he'd just been treated to the female equivalent of the 'wham-bam thank you, ma'am' routine.

He guessed he ought to be hurt, but first he'd have to get over the shock.

Not that he hadn't been dumped before, mind you. Of course he had. He could still recall Mary O'Halloran, slapping him down in front of all his mates when he'd been thirteen and full of the carelessness of youth. He'd snogged her and forgotten to call her the next day so he figured he'd deserved it. In fact, he still felt a little guilty whenever he thought about Mary.

But even Mary, riled to the hilt, hadn't dumped him without chewing his ear off first for twenty minutes about all his shortcomings. And he'd never met a woman since who wouldn't talk you to death about 'the state of the relationship' as soon as look at you. God, when he thought about all the times Rachel had insisted on 'having a little chat about where they were headed' his stomach sank.

So why should he care that Daisy had brushed off his offer to talk? Sure, he hadn't really meant it. All he'd wanted to do was calm her down, get her to stick around.

He lay on the bed, the ripples of sexual fulfilment making him feel lethargic, and tried to convince himself it was all for the best. He should be overjoyed. It made things a lot less complicated. He wasn't looking for anything serious and neither was she.

He rubbed his belly, stretched his legs under the sheet, contemplated taking another shower, then caught the heady whiff of her scent. Heat surged into his crotch. He frowned and sat up, staring at the tent forming in his lap.

The damn problem was, he wasn't pleased. Because he wasn't finished with her yet. Okay, they had nothing in common, and their one-night stand, or one-morning stand or whatever the hell it was didn't have any future. But still, he hadn't wanted it to end, not yet. He'd had plans for today. Fine, so them getting naked and having mind-blowing sex hadn't been a definite part of it, but he didn't see why they shouldn't go with the flow there. They might not be compatible out of bed, but they sure as hell were in it. In fact they were more than compatible. She'd been as blown away as he had by the intensity of…

He stopped, his brain finally catching up with his indignation. Had she been spooked by how good they were together? He relaxed back into the pillow, the pounding heat in his groin finally starting to subside.

That had to be the problem. Daisy might be the most pragmatic, forthright woman he'd ever met, but she was still a girl. And wasn't it just like a girl to analyse everything to death? To worry about what great sex meant instead of just enjoying it while it lasted.

He huffed out a laugh.

And now he thought about it, he didn't have to feel hard done by either. Little Daisy might turn out to be his ideal woman. Someone sexy enough to turn him inside out with lust and smart enough to know he wasn't a good bet for the long haul. Hell, they'd only just met and she'd already figured that out. Now all he had to do was show her that just because they weren't going to spend the rest of their natural lives together, didn't mean they couldn't spend the next little while exploring their potential in other areas.

He whipped back the sheet and leaped out of bed—his faith in the wonder of womankind restored. He'd have that shower after all, get dressed and then head to her place and invite her back for breakfast. Whatever she had planned for the next couple of days he'd persuade her to drop it.

Daisy seemed to be remarkably susceptible to him— whether she liked it or not. Getting her over this little hump so they could finish what they'd started shouldn't be too tough. He strode into the bathroom, his whistled rendition of 'Molly Malone' echoing off the tiles.

CHAPTER SIX

CONNOR was feeling a lot less jolly two hours later as he stood on Daisy's doorstep. He braced the box under his arm, heard the furious feline hiss from inside and stabbed the door buzzer, impatient to see Daisy again and get at least one thing sorted to his satisfaction.

It had taken him an eternity to chase her landlady's cat down and get it in the box—and he had a criss-cross of scratches on his hand for his trouble. Unfortunately the cat wasn't the only thing that had mucked up his morning. After a panicked call from the architect on his Paris project, he'd had to book a Eurostar ticket for this afternoon.

As soon as he'd put the phone down to his PA, Danny had been on the line from Manhattan, begging him to bring his trip there forward a week to stave off the now apparently imminent possibility of the Melrose project going belly up. He really hadn't needed another conversation about Danny's ludicrous 'fake fiancée' solution so he'd ended up agreeing to fly over there from Paris at the end of the week.

All of which was going to stall his plans to get the delicious Daisy Dean back in his bed any time soon. But once he'd finally wrestled the cat into the box, he'd made up his mind he wasn't prepared to write the idea off completely. Not yet.

He glanced at his watch. He knew a cosy little four-star restaurant in Notting Hill where he and Daisy could discuss their next moves over a glass of Pouilly Fumé and some seared scallops before he grabbed a cab to St Pancras International. He didn't see why he shouldn't stake his claim before he went. A three-week wait would be a pain, but he could handle it if he had something tangible to look forward to when he got back.

He pressed the buzzer again. Where the hell was she? It was ten o'clock on a Saturday morning and she'd been up most of the night—surely she couldn't have gone out?

He noticed the ragged paint on the huge oak door and glanced up at the house's elegant Georgian frontage. Crumbling brickwork and rotting window sills proved the place had been sadly neglected for years. She really did live in a dump.

The thought brightened his mood considerably.

Maybe he could persuade her to housesit while he was gone. He'd had a call back from the estate agent while he was having his spat with the cat. Even if he got an offer straight away as the guy seemed to think, it would take a bit to do all the paperwork. And he liked the idea of Daisy being there, waiting for him when he got back from his trip. He was just imagining how much they could enjoy his homecoming when the door swung open.

'Well, if it isn't the invisible neighbour.' The elderly woman standing on the threshold stared down her nose at him, which was quite a feat considering she was at least a foot shorter than he was. The voluminous silk dressing gown with feather trim she wore looked like something out of a vintage Hollywood movie. Her small birdlike frame and the wisps of white hair peeking out of her matching silk turban would have made her look fragile, but for her regal stature and the sharp intelligence in her gaze. Which was currently boring several holes in his hide.

'What do *you* want?' she sneered, eyeing him as if he were a piece of rotting meat. 'Finally come to introduce yourself, have you?'

As Connor didn't know the woman, he figured she must have mistaken him for someone else. 'The name's Connor Brody. I've a cat with me belongs to the landlady here.'

He put the box down in front of her, the screech from inside making his ears throb and the slashes on his hand sting.

She gasped and clutched a hand to her breast as her face softened. 'You've found Mr Pootles?' she whispered, tears seeping over her lids. She bent over the box—the anticipation on her face as bright as that of a child on Christmas morning.

He stepped forward, about to warn her she was liable to get her hand ripped off, but stopped when she prised open the lid and a deep purr resonated from inside. He watched astonished as she scooped the devil cat into her arms. Lucifer rubbed its head under her chin, gave another satisfied purr and slanted him a smug look. The little suck-up.

'How can I ever thank you, young man?' The old woman straightened, clutching devil cat to her bosom as if it were her firstborn babe. 'You've made an old lady very happy.' The joyful tears sheening her whiskey-brown eyes and the softening of her facial features made her look about twenty years younger. 'Wherever did you find him? We've been searching for weeks.'

'The cat's been bunking in my kitchen,' he said, stuffing his hands in his pockets, not sure he really deserved her thanks. 'I should warn you. There's more than one cat now.'

The elderly lady's eyes popped wide. 'Oh?'

He nodded at the creature, who was gazing at him as if butter wouldn't melt in its mouth. 'Your Mr Pootles became a mammy eleven days ago. I have four kittens at mine.'

'Four…' The lady gasped and then giggled, sounding for all the world like a sixteen-year-old girl. She held the cat up in front of her and nuzzled it. 'You naughty cat. Why didn't you tell me you were a girl?'

Connor figured it probably wasn't his place to point out the cat couldn't talk. 'Here.' He pulled out a spare set of keys from his pocket. 'You'll want these to get the kittens now, as they're too little to be on their own for long.'

'Why, that's awfully sweet of you,' she said, taking the keys.

'They're in a cupboard in the kitchen,' he added. 'Is Daisy around?' he asked, awkwardly. 'I need to speak to her.'

The old lady's eyes widened as she put the keys in the pocket of her gown. 'You know Daisy?' she asked, sounding a lot more astonished about that than she had been about her tomcat's kittens.

'Sure, we're friends,' he said, colour rising in his cheeks under the old woman's scrutiny. It wasn't a lie. If what they'd got up to that morning didn't make them friends, he didn't know what did.

'Well, I never did,' she said. 'After all the nonsense Daisy's said about you in the last few weeks.'

What nonsense? She hadn't even met him until last night.

'Daisy's such a dark horse.' The old woman gave him a confidential grin, confusing him even more. 'I always thought she might have a little crush on you, the way she could not stop talking about you. Little did I know she'd been fooling us all along. So, did you two have a lovers' tiff? Is that why she said all those awful things?'

'No,' he said, totally clueless now. And not liking the feeling one bit. 'What things?'

The old woman waved her hand dismissively. 'Oh, you know Daisy. She's always got an opinion and she does love to voice it. She told us all how you were rich and arrogant and far too self-absorbed to care about a missing cat. But we know that's not true now, don't we?'

Connor's lips flattened into a grim line. So she'd bad-mouthed him, had she, and before she'd even met him. Wasn't that always the way of it? As a boy it had driven him insane when people who barely knew him told him he'd never amount to a thing. That he'd turn out no better than his Da.

But Daisy's bad opinion didn't just make him mad. It hurt a little too. Which made him more mad. Why should it bother him what some small-minded, silly little English girl thought?

Was that why she'd bolted? Because she'd decided he

wasn't good enough for her? If she thought that she was in for a surprise.

'Is Daisy in her room? I need to speak to her.' *Make that yell at her.*

'Of course not, dear,' the old lady said quizzically. 'Daisy and Juno are working on The Funky Fashionista.'

'The what?'

The woman gave him a curious look. 'Her stall in Portobello Market.'

'Right you are,' he said hastily. Not knowing what Daisy did for a living probably made his claim to be a friend look a bit suspect. He took a step down the stairs, keen to get away.

Portobello Road Market was round the corner. It shouldn't take him too long to track her down—and give her a good piece of his mind.

'But, Mr Brody…' The elderly woman called him back. 'How will I get your keys back to you?'

'Don't worry about them,' he said, a smile playing across his lips as the kernel of an idea began to form. 'You keep them. If I lock myself out, it'll be useful for you to have a set.'

He waved and hopped down the last few steps to the pavement.

He mulled his idea over as he strode down the street towards the Bello. And the more he mulled, the more irresistible the idea became. Sure what he had in mind was outrageous, and Daisy wasn't going to like it one bit, if her disappearing act that morning was anything to go by. But if ever there was a way to kill two birds with one stone, and teach a certain little English girl how not to throw said stones in glass houses, this had to be it.

After the shoddy way she'd treated him, it was the least she deserved.

Daisy Dean owed him. And what he had in mind would make the payback all the sweeter.

CHAPTER SEVEN

'NO WONDER you're knackered. It's called compassion fatigue.' Juno scowled as she placed the last of Daisy's new batch of silk-screen printed scarves at the front of the stall. 'You didn't need to spend the whole night there looking after him. You don't owe that guy a thing. And I bet he didn't even thank you for it.'

Oh, yes, he did.

The heat suffused Daisy's cheeks as she recalled how thoroughly Connor Brody had thanked her. She ducked behind the rack of cotton dresses and prayed Juno hadn't noticed her reaction.

'Why are you blushing?'

Daisy peeked over the top of the rack to see Juno watching her. Did the woman have radar or something? 'I'm not blushing. I'm rearranging the dress sizes.' She popped back behind the rack. 'It never ceases to amaze me how out of order they get,' she babbled, shoving a size fourteen in between two size eights.

'Daze, did something happen I should know about?' Juno asked quietly, appearing beside her. She placed her hand over the one Daisy had clutching the rack. 'If he did something to you, you can talk to me—you know that, right?'

The concern in Juno's eyes made Daisy's blush get a whole lot worse as embarrassment was comprehensively replaced by guilt.

It had taken her less than twenty minutes of angst after bolting out of Connor Brody's house that morning to get over her panic attack. She wasn't even sure what she'd got so worked up about now. Okay, so she'd jumped him, but who wouldn't in her situation? She'd been exhausted. She'd spent the whole night in close proximity to that beautiful body of his. She'd seen him at his most vulnerable plagued by those terrible nightmares and it had created a false sense of intimacy. So what? He hadn't exactly objected when she'd demanded he make love to her. And she'd never be idiotic or delusional enough to fall in love with a man like Connor Brody. A man who was so totally the opposite of the nice, calm, settled, steady, average guy she needed.

All of which meant she could rest assured that what had happened in Connor Brody's bed that morning hadn't suddenly turned her into her mother. Because that had always been her mother's mistake—not the pursuit of good sex, but the belief that good sex meant you must have found the man of your dreams. Daisy knew that good sex—even stupendous sex—had nothing whatsoever to do with love.

The relief she'd felt had been immense.

But the one thing Daisy hadn't been able to get past—or to justify—was the scurrilous way she'd treated Connor Brody. Not just after they'd made love—but before she'd ever met him. Was it any wonder Juno thought something bad had happened at Brody's house when Daisy had spent the last few weeks assassinating his character to anyone who would listen?

And on what evidence? None at all. She'd judged him and condemned him because he was rich and good-looking and, if she was being perfectly honest with herself, because she'd fancied him right from the first time she'd laid eyes on him and she'd resented it.

She'd broken into his home, all but accused him of killing a cat he'd actually been looking after and then—after trying to make amends during the night by nursing him through his fever—she'd ruined it all by seducing him first thing the following morning and then freaking out and running off.

Thinking about the way she'd brushed off his perfectly sweet attempts to calm her down made her cringe. He'd been a nice guy about the whole thing—had even offered to talk about it, and how many guys did that after a one-night stand? And what had she done? She'd told him to get lost. The poor guy probably thought she was a total basketcase and frankly who could blame him?

Daisy gave a deep sigh. At the very least she owed the man an apology. What was that old saying about pride going before a fall? She might as well have hurled herself off a cliff.

'Daze, you're really starting to worry me.' Juno's urgent voice pulled Daisy out of her musings. 'Tell me what he did. If he's hurt you, I'll make him pay. I promise.'

Daisy gave a half-smile, amused despite everything at the thought of Juno, who was even shorter than she was, going toe to toe with Brody. She shook her head. 'He didn't hurt me, Ju. He's a nice bloke.'

She paused. Maybe *nice* was too tame a word to describe Connor Brody, but it served its purpose here. 'If anything, it's the other way around—I hurt him.'

She knew she hadn't done more than dent his pride a little, but that still made her feel bad.

Walking round the stall, Daisy pinged open the drawer on the antique cash register. She lifted out the rolls of change and began cracking them open.

'How?' Juno asked, picking up a five-pence roll and ripping off the paper wrapping.

Daisy blew out a breath. 'I've been a complete cow to him. All those things I said to you and Mrs V and everyone else, all the assumptions I made. They all turned out to be a load of old cobblers.' The tinkle of change hitting the cash drawer's wooden base couldn't disguise the shame in her voice.

'What makes you think he'd care?' Juno scoffed, but then

she'd always been willing to think the worst of any good-looking guy. Daisy wondered when she'd started to adopt the same prejudices.

'That's not the point,' Daisy said. 'I care.'

'All you really said was that he's rich and arrogant. What's so awful about that?'

'He may be rich, but he's not arrogant.' As she said it Daisy recalled the way he'd kissed her senseless before she'd even woken up properly. 'All right, maybe he is a little bit arrogant, but I expect he's used to women falling at his feet.' She certainly had.

'So what? That doesn't give him the right to take advantage—'

Daisy pressed her fingers to Juno's lips. 'He didn't take advantage of me. What happened was entirely consensual.' Just thinking about how consensual it had been was making her pulse skitter.

'What exactly *did* happen?' Juno's eyes narrowed. 'Because it's beginning to sound as if more than rest and recuperation were involved. You're not telling me you slept with him, are you?'

Daisy's flush flared back to life at the accusatory look in Juno's eyes. How on earth was she going to explain her behaviour to Juno when it had taken her so long to explain it to herself? She opened her mouth to say something, anything, when the rumble of a deep Irish accent had both their heads whipping round to the front of the stall.

'Hello, ladies.'

Daisy's heartbeat skipped a beat. He looked tall and devastating in the same worn T-shirt and jeans he'd stripped out of that morning—and amused. His lips twitched in that sensual smile she remembered a little too vividly from the moment she'd woken up in his bedroom.

'While I hate to interrupt this fascinating bit of chit-chat—' he gripped the top of the stall's canopy and leaned over the brightly coloured scarves and blouses '—I'd like to have a word, Daisy.' His forefinger skimmed her cheek. 'In private.'

Daisy swallowed, feeling the burn where the calloused fingertip had touched.

'Daisy's busy. Buzz off.'

He dropped his hand and shifted his gaze to Juno, still looking amused. 'Who would you be, then? Daisy's keeper?'

'Maybe I am?' Juno blustered, standing on tiptoe and thrusting her chin out—which made her look like a midget with a Napoleonic complex next to Brody's tall, relaxed frame. 'And who the hell are you? Mr High and—'

Daisy slapped her hand over Juno's mouth.

· 'It's all right, Ju,' she whispered, desperate to shut her friend up. 'I'll take it from here.'

All she needed now was for Brody to get an inkling of what she'd said about him to pretty much the whole neighbourhood. This apology was going to be agonising enough, without Juno and her attitude wading in and making it ten times worse.

'I'll explain everything later,' she said into Juno's ear, holding her hand over her friend's mouth. 'Can you look after the stall on your own for half an hour?'

Daisy took Juno's muffled grunt as a yes and let her go.

'Fine,' Juno grumbled. She shot Brody a mutinous look. 'But if you're not back by then I'm coming after you.'

Daisy gave Juno a quick nod. Great, she guessed she'd owe Juno an apology too before this was over. She picked up her bag and rounded the stall to join Brody. Right at the moment, though, she had rather bigger fish to fry.

'I know a café round the corner in Cambridge Gardens,' she murmured, walking through the few milling shoppers who'd already made it up to the far end of the market under the Westway where The Funky Fashionista was situated.

He fell into step beside her but said nothing.

'Why don't we go there?' she continued, not quite able to look at him. 'They do great cappuccinos.'

And Gino's cosy little Italian coffee house was also off the tourist track enough that it shouldn't be too crowded yet. The last thing she wanted was an audience while she choked down her monster helping of humble pie.

It took them less than five minutes to get to Gino's. Not surprising given that Daisy jogged most of the way, clinging onto her bag with both hands and making sure she kept a couple of steps ahead of Brody's long stride. As soon as they'd walked away from the stall she'd been consumed by panic at the possibility that he might touch her or speak to her before she'd figured out what she was going to say to him.

And how ridiculous was that? she thought as they strolled into Gino's and she grabbed the first booth by the door. He'd been buried deep inside her less than three hours ago, given her the most earth-shattering orgasm of her life and now she was scared to even look at him.

She slid into the booth and hastily dumped her bag onto the vinyl-bench seat beside her, blocking off any thoughts he might have of sitting next to her. Casting his eyes at the bag, he slid his long body onto the bench opposite. As he rested his arms loosely on the table she noticed the Boston Celtics logo ripple across his chest.

Her eyes flicked away.

Don't even go there, you silly woman. Hasn't that chest got you in enough trouble already?

She raised her hand to salute Gino, who was standing behind the counter. 'Would you like a cappuccino?' she asked as she watched Gino wave back and grab his pad.

'What I'd like is for you to look at me.'

The dry comment forced her to meet his eyes.

'That's better,' he said, the low murmur deliberately intimate. 'Was that so terrible now?'

Daisy decided to ignore the patronising tone. She supposed she deserved it.

'Look, Mr Brod… I mean, Connor. I've got something to say and I…' She rushed the words and then came to a complete stop, her tongue stalling on the apology she'd worked out.

Then Gino stepped up to the booth. 'Hello, Daisy luv. What'll it be? The usual?'

Daisy stared blankly at her friend, struggling for a second to remember what her usual was. 'No, thanks, no muffin today.' She'd probably choke on it. 'Just a latte, not too heavy on the froth.'

'As always, my lovely,' Gino said as he jotted the order on his pad, his broad cockney accent belying the swarthy Italian colouring he'd inherited from his mother. 'What's your poison, mate?' he asked, addressing Brody.

'Espresso.'

'Coming right up,' Gino replied. Then to Daisy's consternation he tucked his pad under his arm and offered Brody his hand. 'Gino Jones, by the way. This is my place,' he said as Brody shook it. 'Haven't seen you in here before. What's your name?'

Daisy rolled her eyes. She'd forgotten what a busybody Gino could be.

'Connor Brody,' Brody replied. 'I moved in next door to Daisy a few weeks back.'

Gino frowned, releasing Brody's hand. 'You're not the bloke who—'

Daisy coughed loudly. Good God, had she blabbed to Gino about Brody too? Why did she have such a big mouth? 'Actually, we're in a hurry, Gee,' she said, slanting Gino her 'shut up, you idiot' look. 'I've left Ju alone on the stall and the market will be heaving soon.'

'No sweat,' Gino said carefully. 'I'll go get your drinks.' Then he shot her his 'don't think I won't ask you about this guy later' look and left.

'You know, it's funny,' Brody said, although he didn't sound at all amused, 'but people around here don't like me much.' The statement sounded slightly disingenuous, but Daisy suspected that was wishful thinking on her part.

Her stomach sank to the soles of her shoes as guilt consumed her.

Time to stop messing about and give the man the apology she owed him. And she better make it a good one.

'Mr… Sorry, Connor.' She stalled again, forced herself to continue. 'I've behaved pretty badly. Climbing into your garden, accusing you of…' She paused. *Don't say you thought he killed the cat, you twerp.* 'Of not helping to find Mrs V's cat. And then…' The blush was back with a vengeance as he watched her, his face impassive. 'This morning I forced you to make love to me. And then I ran off without saying goodbye. I feel completely ashamed of my behaviour… It was incredibly tacky and I'm awfully sorry. And I'd like to make it up to you.' She stumbled to a stop, not sure what else to say.

His expression had barely changed throughout her whole rambling speech. Maybe he'd looked a little surprised at first, but then his face had taken on this inscrutable mask.

'Hmm,' he said, the sound rumbling up through his chest. For some strange reason, Daisy's knees began to shake. She crossed her legs.

He cocked his head to one side. 'That's a lot of sins you've to make up.'

'I know,' she said, hoping she sounded suitably contrite.

To her surprise, he reached across the table and took her hand in his, threading his fingers through hers. 'What makes you think I was being forced, Daisy Dean? Did it seem to you I wasn't enjoying myself?'

She gulped past the dryness tightening her throat. How had they got onto this topic? 'No, it's not that. It's just. I was rather demanding. I don't think I gave you much of a choice in the matter.'

She ought to tug her fingers away, but somehow they'd got tangled up in his. Just as her stomach was now tangled in knots.

He rubbed his thumb across her palm, making her fingers curl into his. 'You'd be wrong about that,' he said. 'You gave me a choice and I took it. With a great deal of enthusiasm.'

His thumb began stroking her wrist, doing appalling things to her pulse rate. She was just about to muster the will to pull her hand away when he let her go and sat back.

Gino cleared his throat loudly and slid their coffees onto the table.

'Here you go, folks.' Gino sent Daisy a searching look, raising his eyebrows pointedly, before leaving them alone.

No doubt Gino was as confused as she was. Why had she been holding Brody's hand? Letting him caress her like that? It wasn't as if they were intimate. Well, not in the proper sense.

She wrapped her hands around her coffee mug to keep them out of harm's way. 'I'm so glad there are no hard feelings,' she said.

At least she would be glad, once she'd got away from that penetrating gaze.

'Not about making love to you, no,' he said, the Irish in his voice brushing over her like an aphrodisiac. 'There are no hard feelings about that. I enjoyed it, a lot. And, I think, so did you.' It wasn't a question. 'But as to the rest,' he continued. 'There you've more explaining to do.'

Her cup clattered onto the table and coffee slurped over the rim. 'I do?'

'Why did you run off?'

'I don't know,' she lied, and then felt guilty again when he lifted one dark brow. He wasn't buying it.

'It was a bit too intense,' she said. 'And I don't usually jump into bed with men I hardly know.' She clamped her mouth shut. Half the truth would have to do. Because she was getting the weird sensation she was being toyed with, lured into some kind of a trap. Which was preposterous, of course, but Daisy never ignored her instincts.

'That's good to know,' he said.

She took a gulp of the hot coffee and then reached for her bag. 'I'm so glad we got all this settled. I'd hate for us not to be friends. Especially as you live right next door.'

Which made the whole thing even more awful. How was she going to face him every day if her hormones went into meltdown every time she looked at him? She'd have to get that little problem under control and quickly. But for now she decided distance was probably the best medicine. Slinging her bag over her shoulder, she slid out of the booth and offered her hand. 'I'll see you around. The coffees are on me. I'll tell Gino to put them on my tab. Thanks for being so understanding.'

He clasped her hand, the warm, rough feel of his palm sending little shivers up her arm—and held on. 'Sit down. We're not finished.'

'We're not?'

He nodded at the booth seat. 'There's still the matter of the making up to settle.'

'What?' She plopped back in her seat, not at all sure she liked the commanding tone.

'The making up.'

Finally he let her hand go. She tucked it under the table, her fingers tingling.

'You said you wanted to make up for what you'd done,' he said calmly. 'And we're going to have to sort it now, because I don't have much time.' He looked at his watch. 'I'm catching the Eurostar to Paris in a little over an hour. I've got eight days there and then I'll be two weeks in New York.'

Daisy's shoulders slumped with relief. Thank you, God. She had no idea why he was telling her his itinerary, but at least she'd have over three weeks before she had to see him again. She should be well over this silly chemical reaction by then. 'That's wonderful. I'm sure you'll have a lovely time. I'll miss you,' she added, a tad concerned to realise it was the truth.

'Not for long, you won't,' he said, the predatory smile that tugged at his lips concerning her a whole lot more. 'Because when I get to New York you'll be meeting me there.'

She choked out a laugh. 'You lost me,' she said, but she could have sworn she heard the sound of a trap snapping shut.

He relaxed back in his seat, the picture of self-satisfaction. 'You want to make things up to me,' he prompted. 'It so happens I need a girlfriend in New York for those two weeks. It has to do with a business deal.' He tapped his fingers on the table in a rhythm that sounded like the tumblers of a lock clicking into place. 'And that girlfriend's going to be you.'

He could not be serious? Was he insane? 'Don't be ridiculous. I'm not going to New York. When I said I wanted to make things up to you, I was planning to bake you another plate of brownies. Not take a two-week trip to New York as your fake date. Are you nuts?' He was still looking at her with that cocksure, you'll-do-as-you're-told expression on his face. It was starting to annoy her. 'Even if I wanted to go.' Which she most definitely did not. 'I couldn't possibly. I've got my stall to run.'

He sighed. 'If your little bodyguard friend can't run the stall on her own you can find someone to help her. I'll pay any wages due. My PA will sort out your travel plans.' He looked pointedly at his watch again, as if to say, *I don't have time for this.*

Daisy's temper kicked up another notch. 'You're not listening to me, Brody. I'm not doing it. I don't want to. You'll have to find someone else.' She did not want to spend two weeks alone with him in New York. She already knew how irresistible he was—what if she had another lapse in judgment brought on by extreme hormonal overload and jumped him again? Things could get very complicated indeed. 'I don't owe you that much,' she finished, indignation seeping from every pore.

'Oh, but you do, Daisy Dean.' He leaned forward, those icy

blue eyes chilling her to the bone. 'You told half of London I was selfish, arrogant and not to be trusted. That's known as slander.'

The blood seeped out of her face. How did he know about that?

'There happen to be laws against that sort of thing. So unless you want me to be calling my solicitor, you'd best be on that plane.'

He got up from the booth. She drew back, but he caught her chin in his fingers and tilted her face to his. 'And, Daisy,' he murmured, the warmth of his breath making her heart go into palpitations. 'Who said anything about a fake date?' he finished, his lips so close she could all but feel them pressed against hers.

'But I'm not your girlfriend,' she managed to say as her heart pounded in her throat. 'I certainly don't love you. And right now I don't even like you.'

His gaze swept over her, making her notice the length of his lashes again, before his eyes fixed on her face. If she'd hoped to wound him she could see by his expression she'd failed.

'Make no mistake. This is only a two-week deal. I'm not in the market for anything more and neither are you.'

She thought she could hear a tinge of regret in his voice and cursed her overactive imagination. She doubted he had the emotional capacity for regret. The rat.

'But we don't have to love each other for what I have in mind.'

With that, his lips came down on hers in a hard, fast and sinfully sexy kiss. She tried to twist away but he held her firm until she felt the pulse of response, the throb of heat. And before she knew what was happening, she was kissing him back.

He pulled his mouth away first and straightened. 'You like me right enough, Daisy Dean.' He brushed his thumb across her bottom lip. 'And we both know it.'

She jerked back, mute with anger and humiliated right down to her knickers—which were now soaked with need.

'There will be lots we can see and do in Manhattan—and I've a mind to show it to you,' he continued, that devil-may-care charm not the least bit fazed by her furious glare. 'So, you can spend the two weeks in your bed alone, or make the most of the experience. The choice will be yours.' He gave her a mock salute. 'I'll see you in New York, Angel Face.'

Daisy glared at his back as he strolled out of the café, heard him whistling some off-key Irish ditty as he disappeared down the street.

The overbearing, conceited, blackmailing jerk.

She flung her bag on the seat. How dared he steamroll her like that?

She glowered at the booth opposite, sure she could feel smoke pumping out of her ears. To think she'd actually felt sorry for what she'd said about him. He wasn't just arrogant. He was a megalomaniac—with an ego the size of his precious Manhattan.

If he thought she was going to step into line, he could forget it. And whatever happened she was not going to sleep with him again. No way, no how.

But even as she made the promise she knew it was going to be next to impossible to keep.

CHAPTER EIGHT

BY THE time Daisy had packed up the stall with Juno that evening and trudged back to her bedsit, she'd decided the conversation with Brody in Gino's café had been his crazy idea of a joke. Either that or she'd been dreaming.

He couldn't be serious about blackmailing her into a trip to New York. This was the twenty-first century—people didn't do that sort of thing. Well, not people with any semblance of decency.

She turned on the light and toed off her shoes, every cell in her body weeping with exhaustion after a virtually sleepless night and ten solid hours on her feet—not to mention the day's emotional trauma. Thank you so very much, Connor Brody. Pulling off the bangles on her wrist, she dropped them into her jewellery box, then sat on the bed and unclipped her silver ankle bracelet. She'd just forget the whole ridiculous episode.

She hadn't even told Juno about Brody's threat. She'd forced herself to calm down before returning to the stall—her lips still red and puffy from Brody's goodbye kiss—and had put a few things in perspective. Brody could not possibly have been serious. So why bother Juno with the details?

Edging her curtain back, Daisy peeked at the windows of Brody's house. Pitch black. Thank goodness. He must be in Paris. She huffed. Good riddance.

She let the curtain drop, lay down on the bed and stared at

the fairy-tale motif she'd painted on the ceiling last winter. A blue-eyed, black-haired cherub winked at her cheekily from behind a moonbeam.

She shifted onto her side and tucked her hands under her cheek—the damn cherub reminding her of someone she did not want to be reminded of.

Sunday and Monday flew by in a flurry of work and other related activities. Daisy manned the stall, ran a class on silk-screen printing at the local community centre, got stuck into her latest clothes designs and did her regular slot at the Notting Hill Arts Project—happily getting neck-deep in tissue paper, glitter and PVA glue as she helped her group of five- to ten-year-olds make their costumes for this year's Notting Hill Carnival. Just as she'd suspected, there had been no word from Brody. By Tuesday night, the events of the weekend had been as good as forgotten—give or take a few luridly erotic dreams.

Bright and way too early Wednesday morning, her three days of denial came to an abrupt end.

'Daisy, Daisy, open up, dear.' Mrs Valdermeyer's excited voice was punctuated by several loud raps on the door. 'A package has arrived for you. Special delivery no less.'

Daisy rolled over, blinking the sleep out of her eyes. Stumbling out of bed, she checked the Mickey Mouse clock on the mantelpiece and groaned. It was still shy of seven a.m.

She pulled the door open and her landlady whisked past, holding a small brown-paper parcel aloft like a waiter on silver-service duty. She laid it ceremonially on the bed. Then turned to Daisy and bounced up on her toes.

'Isn't it exciting?' She clapped her hands. 'It's from that handsome young man next door—it says so on the front.'

Daisy felt a much louder groan coming on, but bit it back.

'What's going on?' Juno stood in the doorway, wearing her Bugs Bunny pyjamas and a sleepy frown.

'Daisy has a package from a gentleman admirer. Isn't it

exciting?' Mrs Valdermeyer plopped down on the bed and patted a spot next to her. 'Come in, Juno, and let's watch her open it.'

Daisy felt the groan start to strangle her. Fabulous. When had her bedroom become package-opening central?

'What gentleman admirer?' Juno asked. Walking into the room, she glanced at the package. 'Oh, him,' she scoffed.

Daisy opened her mouth to speak—and start ushering her audience out the door—when Mrs V interrupted her. 'Don't be such a grump, Juno dear.' She whisked a pair of scissors out of her dressing gown with a flourish. 'The man is positively delicious and he saved Mrs Pootles from a fate worse than death. Daisy could do a lot worse.' She offered Daisy the scissors. 'In fact Daisy did do a lot worse—remember that awful Gary?'

'Do I ever,' Juno replied, sitting next to Mrs Valdermeyer. She caught Daisy's eye. 'But I'm not sure this guy is that big an improvement.'

'Well, he's certainly a lot better looking,' Mrs Valdermeyer shot back.

'We're not dating, Mrs V,' Daisy interceded, before her landlady got totally the wrong idea. 'So there's no need—'

'Why ever not, dear? He's loaded, you know. Which, I might add, comes in very handy if the passion fades.'

Daisy grabbed the scissors, resigned to opening the package as quickly as possible before the conversation deteriorated any further.

She snipped the string and folded the paper back carefully, aware of the two pairs of eyes watching every move she made. Her heart pummelled as she opened the lid.

Please don't let him have put crotchless knickers in here. Or something equally tacky.

But as she upended the box she was surprised to see three envelopes of varying sizes and a slim, black velvet case bounce onto the bed.

'How marvellous. Jewellery. Open that last, Daisy,' Mrs

Valdermeyer said, thrusting the first of the envelopes into Daisy's hand. 'Jewellery needs to be properly savoured.'

Once Daisy had opened all three of the envelopes, Mrs Valdermeyer was practically doing cartwheels around the room and Juno's frown had turned into the San Andreas fault.

Daisy slumped onto the bed, stunned. In her lap she had a first-class return ticket to JFK dated for twelve noon that coming Sunday, a carefully typed itinerary of her travel arrangements signed by someone called Caroline Prestwick and a gold credit card in her name.

Her hand shook as Mrs Valdermeyer thrust the jewellery case into her lap on top of the other booty. Daisy picked it up, and found another envelope attached to the bottom of the case.

She ripped it off, stared blankly at her name scrawled on the front in large, block letters and then tore it open. Inside was a sheet of thick textured white paper with the Brody Construction logo stamped across the top. As she scanned the contents of the letter her fingers began to tremble.

Angel Face,

I found the sparkles in Paris and thought they would suit. Get anything else you need with the card—and don't spare yourself. I want you to look the part.

There's a car booked for the airport. See you at The Waldorf.

Connor
PS: I've my solicitor on speed-dial if you don't show.

'It's all so wonderfully romantic,' Mrs Valdermeyer crooned over her shoulder. 'Two weeks at The Waldorf *and* a gold credit card. You're going to have the time of your life, Daisy.'

'What does he mean about his solicitor?' Juno said.

'I'm not going.' Daisy folded the letter and shoved it back

in its envelope. She couldn't possibly go. Okay, somewhere in the last few days she'd got over her anger, and for a moment Mrs Valdermeyer's industrial-strength enthusiasm had almost blinded her to the truth. For a split second she'd seen herself on Connor's arm decked out in glitters and her best posh frock. She'd never been further than Calais on a school trip so she felt she was entitled to get momentarily carried away. But she couldn't do it. And what had he meant by 'I want you to look the part'—as if she were his personal mannequin? The cheek of the man.

'Of course you're going, my dear. Don't be absurd,' Mrs Valdermeyer said.

'I really don't think she should,' Juno piped up. 'She'd be totally at his mercy and—'

'Stop right there, Juno.' Mrs Valdermeyer got up and took Juno's arm. 'I want you out of here. Daisy and I have to talk about this in private,' she said, dragging Juno to the door.

Before Juno had a chance to say anything else, she'd been shoved over the threshold and had the door slammed at her back.

Mrs Valdermeyer brushed her hands together. 'Right, now the most unromantic woman in the Western World has gone, let's discuss this properly.'

She sat down next to Daisy, laid a hand on her knee.

'You don't understand.' Daisy fisted her fingers on Connor's perfunctory letter. 'It's not romantic at all. He just needs a girlfriend to hang on his arm for a couple of weeks. We're not even dating. It's a business thing. Or something.' She let out a trembling breath. The truth was, he thought so little of her, he hadn't even had the courtesy to tell her why exactly he needed her there.

Daisy shoved Connor's letter and the jeweller's case back in the box—ignoring the cold fingers of regret gripping her stomach.

How pathetic that she felt depressed she couldn't go. She was her own woman, she didn't need a man to complete her and she certainly didn't need some too-sexy-by-half egoma-niac sweeping her off her feet only to dump her back down to earth again two weeks later.

'He may very well think that,' Mrs Valdermeyer said gently, resting her knarled hand over Daisy's. 'But I suspect there's a bit more to it.'

Tears pricked Daisy's lids—and made her feel even more pathetic. 'Like what?' she said, cynicism sharpening her voice.

'Daisy, dear. Men don't ask a woman on a first-class, all-expenses-paid trip to New York just for the sake of a business deal.'

'He didn't ask me,' Daisy said, the tears she was busy ignoring clogging her throat. 'He told me. And I think he's expecting some pleasure mixed in with his business to justify the expense.'

Mrs Valdermeyer chuckled fondly. 'He is a scoundrel, isn't he? Just like my third husband, Jerry.' She patted Daisy's leg, still chuckling. 'But once you've tamed him, my dear, you'll see they're the very best kind. Both in bed and out.'

Daisy tried to smile at the old lady's irascible tone, but somehow she couldn't muster more than a strained grimace. 'I don't want to tame him. Believe me, it would involve far too much work.'

Mrs Valdermeyer took Daisy's hands in hers. 'Look at me, dear.' Daisy lifted her eyes, saw that the old woman wasn't smiling any more. 'Don't you think you're taking this a bit too seriously? Surely, this is about a man and a woman having a marvellous adventure together. Nothing more. And you've had far too few adventures in your life to let one as spectacu-lar as this pass you by.'

Daisy huffed. 'That's where you're wrong. I had enough adventures to last me a lifetime before I ever came here.'

'No, you didn't. Those were your mother's adventures. They don't count. This is going to be your adventure and you're going to enjoy every minute of it. You need to get out there and experience life before you can think about finding love, you know.'

A flutter of butterfly wings began to beat under Daisy's breastbone. She tired to ignore them. 'I really don't think…'

Mrs Valdermeyer held up her finger to silence her. 'Don't think, Daisy. You're a dear sweet girl who thinks far too much, mostly about everybody but herself. For once, don't think, just feel.' She patted Daisy's knee. 'Take it from me, I'm an old woman and there are a few things I've learned. You've got the rest of your life to plan things out, to do the right thing, to be cautious and careful and responsible. That's what you have to do when you start a family—that's what your mother should have done and didn't. And if you find the right man to do it with it won't be boring, let me tell you. But you're young, and free and single and you get to be spontaneous now, to live life as it comes and take whatever fun and excitement you can grab.' She picked up the velvet jeweller's case. 'Now, I want to know what sparkles your handsome scoundrel picked out for you in Paris. Don't you?'

Mrs Valdermeyer placed the case back in Daisy's lap.

Daisy stared at the embossed gold lettering on the top, ran her finger over the textured velvet. She sighed. What the heck. What harm could it do to take a quick peek? She lifted the heavy case in one hand and opened the lid.

The sight of the emeralds winking on a lattice of silver chains had her heart leaping into her throat and threatening to choke her. She took an unsteady breath and touched the precious stones.

The butterflies went haywire as the fanciful, fairy-tale images that had been hovering at the back of her mind came into sharp, vivid and all-too-real focus.

She could feel the beautiful necklace warming her cleavage, see the luminous satin of a ball gown she'd once designed in her dreams shimmering in the glow of a thousand tiny lights and sense Connor, tall, dark and far too dangerous, his blue eyes bold with appreciation as he held her close in his arms.

She slammed the lid shut like a frantic Pandora with her box.

But the giddy beating of her heart and the heat coiling in her belly told her she was already far too late to seal in the ridiculous dream.

CHAPTER NINE

IF THE days prior to the arrival of Connor's package had gone by in a flurry, the ones afterwards went by in a blur. Once Daisy had faced the fact that she'd have to go to New York—or spend the rest of her life wondering what she might have missed—she became determined to make the absolute most of the opportunity, and avoid all the pitfalls at the same time.

Daisy being Daisy, the practicalities had to be handled first. So she lined up Jacie to help Juno on the stall, finished as much merchandise as she could, rearranged all her community and charity activities and then spent every other spare minute she had working on her wardrobe for the trip. Whether this turned out to be the grandest adventure of her life—or the biggest disaster—she intended to look fabulous. She had her own distinctive style, and whether Connor approved of it or not, she planned to look the part. That would be her part—not his.

As she drew patterns and cut fabrics and stitched and pleated and hemmed and appliquéd late into the night she worked out a basic survival strategy to go with her amazing trousseau.

Whatever happened in New York she would not lose sight of what really mattered. Her life, her career—such as it was—her hopes and dreams for the future did not depend on two thrill-seeking weeks spent in the City That Never Sleeps with a man who had twice as much sex appeal as Casanova and half the depth. As long as she kept her hormones under strict supervision—and didn't succumb to any delusions about true love—she would be absolutely fine.

But despite all Daisy's preparations and pep talks, when Sunday morning arrived, and a black Mercedes with a liveried driver parked in front of the bedsit, the nerves kicked in.

While the chauffeur loaded her suitcase into the boot, she clung onto Mrs V and Juno in a goodbye hug. But as she climbed into the plush leather interior the smell of money and privilege overwhelmed her and the nerves got worse. She wound down the window and gave her friends a shaky wave as the powerful car purred to life and swept away from the kerb.

Once the only home she had ever known was out of sight, she wound the window back up, pressed the button for the air-conditioner and listened to the deafening thumps of her heartbeat over the quiet hum. What on earth had she let herself in for?

She dropped her head back and sighed.

She would be walking into a world she knew nothing about. And throwing herself on the mercy of a guy she knew even less about—not to mention her own surprisingly volatile libido.

She forced herself to take a series of steady breaths as she smoothed the bias-cut sheath dress she'd finished the night before over her knees and felt the pearly silk whisper under her fingertips.

She watched the terraced houses of west London whisk past.

Fine, maybe this would turn out to be the stupidest thing she'd ever done—but at least she'd be doing it in style.

Daisy Dean had never coveted the lifestyles of the rich and famous. She'd never worried about how much money she had, only that she had enough—and she'd been more than happy to work as hard as she had to have the stability she'd always craved.

But as she stepped out of the royal blue limo onto Park Avenue and gazed up at the art deco frontage of The Waldorf Astoria, its gilded-gold filigree glinting in the mid-afternoon sunshine, Daisy had to concede that being rich beyond your wildest dreams might have its uses.

For a girl who'd only ever been on the cheapest of short-haul flights, the journey across the Atlantic—in a leather seat that folded down into a bed bigger than the one she had at home—had been like a dream. She'd cruised above the clouds at thirty thousand feet, sipping champagne and snacking on cordon bleu cuisine—or as much as her nervous tummy would allow—and made herself savour the experience and enjoy it for what it was—a once-in-a-lifetime adventure.

'Ma'am.' The Waldorf's doorman interrupted Daisy's thoughts to hand her a blue ticket. 'Give this to the desk clerk when you check in and we'll have your luggage sent right up to your room.'

'Thank you.' Daisy pulled a ten-dollar bill out of her purse, glad she'd changed some of her own money. But as she offered the tip to the doorman he simply shook his head.

'No need for a gratuity, ma'am. You're Mr Brody's guest. He's already taken care of it.'

'Oh.' Daisy slipped the money back into her purse, her cheeks colouring.

In the last few days she'd been careful not to dwell on her position as 'Mr Brody's guest'. But somehow not even being able to tip the doorman made her feel a bit cheap.

She pushed her uneasiness aside as she made her way up the carpeted stairs to the lobby area. Brody needed her here for his business thingy. She was doing him a favour, so why shouldn't he foot the bill? And she hardly needed to create more problems—she had quite enough on her plate already.

Her breath caught as she took in the huge chandelier hanging over The Waldorf's marbled forecourt and heard the tinkling strains of a Cole Porter song being played on a grand piano in the cocktail bar.

Portobello Road and the Bedsit Co-op suddenly felt a lot more than half a world away.

All leather sofas, vaulted ceilings and dark wood panelling with an ornate carriage clock as its centrepiece, the reception area was no less intimidating. Feeling hopelessly out of place, Daisy approached the desk.

A woman with perfect make-up and an even more perfect smile greeted her. 'What can we do for you today?'

'My name's Daisy Dean. Mr Connor Brody has booked me a room.' The minute the words were out of her mouth, the blush coloured her cheeks again. At least she'd assumed he'd booked her a room. In all the hurried preparations of the last few days and the glamour of the flight, it hadn't even occurred to Daisy to wonder about it. The thought of the kiss they'd shared in Gino's came blasting back to her and the crack he'd made about this not being a 'fake date' and she realised she should have contacted him and clarified their sleeping arrangements. She tried to ignore her pummelling heartbeat. *Don't be silly, Daze, he couldn't possibly be arrogant enough to assume you'll be sleeping together.*

The receptionist tapped a few buttons on her console and smiled. 'You're booked into The Towers Suite with Mr Brody.'

The bottom dropped out of Daisy's stomach. 'Are you sure?' she stuttered.

'Why, yes, of course, Mr Brody made the arrangements personally,' the receptionist continued, apparently oblivious to Daisy's distress. She handed Daisy a thin plastic card in a paper envelope. 'The Towers Suite is on the twenty-first floor,' she said chirpily, pointing to the lifts at the end of the lobby. 'You have a special penthouse elevator for your exclusive use. Mr Brody left a message to say he's in meetings downtown this afternoon, but we're to contact him when you get here and he'll be back at about six o'clock to escort you to dinner.' She smiled again, her teeth so white they gleamed. 'If you have the ticket for your luggage, I'll have it taken to the suite.'

Daisy reached into her bag and handed over the ticket, her

mind whirring. She wanted to demand the receptionist get her another room, but how the heck could she do that when she had a grand total of one hundred dollars in her purse? She'd have to have it out with Brody first, and then insist he get her another room. But the thought of that altercation filled her with dread. She hadn't seen him for over a week, but just the mention of his name had made her thigh muscles clench and her nipples pebble beneath the thin silk of her dress.

'Thanks for your help,' she said, taking the key card in shaking fingers.

She walked to the lift lobby, keeping her back ramrod straight.

Forget feeling cheap, she might as well have had a huge scarlet letter A pasted on her breast.

When Brody finally turned up, she was going to have serious words with him.

After having inspected The Towers Suite, Daisy felt even more intimidated—and like a naive fool.

Taking up most of the twenty-first floor, the suite's rooms were all enormous and luxuriously appointed. Daisy walked through it, her eyes widening until they were the size of dinner plates. Leading off the palatial entrance lobby was a sitting room which boasted a grand piano, a plasma TV the size of a small cinema screen and a lavish balcony with a breathtaking view of the Upper East Side. There were also two walk-in wardrobes and a dressing room, but—surprise, surprise—only one bedroom.

Done out in cream silk wallpaper and matching uphol-stered furnishings, the bedroom had an en-suite bathroom containing a circular whirlpool tub big enough to house an entire rugby team. Daisy had particular trouble breathing though when she got a load of the obscenely large bed. Raised on a dais and covered in a gold satin quilt, it had enough pillows to put a harem to shame.

Of course Brody had just assumed they'd be sleeping together. Why wouldn't he? The man obviously had more money than God, and the arrogance to match. And when you factored in his devastating good looks and that bad-boy Irish charm, she'd bet her bottom dollar no woman had ever said no to him.

She strode back into the bathroom, her annoyance choking her. Twisting the gold-plated taps, she watched the steaming water gush out. Sprinkling in a generous helping of flakes from a heavy glass jar on the vanity, she breathed in the lavender mist and tried to focus on the scent's calming properties. She had a few hours till he arrived at six o'clock. She'd soak out the kinks from the flight, try to relax a little and go over exactly how she was going to handle Brody when he showed up.

CHAPTER TEN

DAISY glanced at the clock on the wall. Still only four-thirty. She closed her eyes, slid into the lavender-scented bubbles and let her mind drift over the classical music coming from the state-of-the-art console in the wall. Despite the battle that loomed large in her future, all the muscles in her body melted into blissful oblivion. When was the last time she'd been able to indulge herself like this? In a place as luxurious as this? Never, that was when.

Ten more minutes of nirvana, that was all she asked, then she'd get ready to face Brody.

She heard a small clicking sound beneath the music and frowned.

'Welcome to New York, angel.'

She shot upright, her eyes flying open as water cascaded onto the floor. 'What are you doing here?' she yelped, wrapping her arms around her naked breasts.

'I live here,' Connor Brody said, the lazy grin spreading as his eyes drifted down.

He stood by the tub, looking tall and gorgeous and intimidating, his hands sunk into the pockets of a charcoal-grey designer suit, a few wisps of chest hair visible above the open collar of his white shirt. She'd never seen him in anything but sweats and jeans and a T-shirt before now. The formal business-wear should have made him look tamer and more sophisticated, but somehow the perfectly tailored fabric had exactly the opposite effect—accentuating the rough, raw masculinity that lay beneath the veneer of civilisation.

And to make matters worse, she was stark naked.

Daisy swallowed heavily, the blast of heat flooding through her coming from more than just the hot bath. She was in serious trouble here.

Those deep blue eyes wandered to her bosom. 'Glad to see you made yourself at home.'

Daisy sank down sharply, splashing more water over the rim, until her chin hit the bubbles. Keeping one arm tight across her breasts, she used the other to shield her sex.

'If you don't mind,' she squeaked, equal parts outrage and mortification, 'I'm having a bath.'

'So I see.' He grinned some more. Then, to her astonishment, he took off his jacket, flung it on the floor, rolled up his shirt sleeves and perched on the edge of the tub.

'What are you doing?' she cried, still squeaking, as he picked up a bar of hotel soap.

Those piercing eyes fixed on her face as he ripped off the soap wrapper, dipped his hands into the water and began lathering the soap in long, tanned fingers. The glint of mischief in his gaze did nothing to diminish the desire.

'Giving you a hand,' he said casually, too casually. The deep husky tone of his voice reverberated across her nerve endings.

She pressed her palm into her sex, struggling to hold back the surge of heat that had made the muscles loosen. 'I don't want a hand.' The breathlessness of the words meant the statement didn't sound as definite as it should.

His lips quirked, as if she'd said something amusing.

He dropped the soap into its bowl and threaded soapy fingers through the hair at her nape. 'Are you sure?' he murmured, reminding her of their first night.

She gasped as his thumb stroked the rapid beat of her pulse and his hand cradled the back of her neck. She braced wet palms against his chest. Water splashed onto the floor as she soaked the front of his shirt. She could see the dark shadow of his chest hair through the damp linen, feel the hard muscles beneath and her arms shook.

He simply laughed and pulled her easily to him as his lips covered hers.

He devoured her mouth, exploring with the strong, insistent strokes of his tongue. The heat geysered up from her core as her fingers curled into the wet fabric. She wanted to shove him away, she really did, but his tongue, his lips were making her light-headed, and every single nerve in her body was throbbing with need. He let her go abruptly and stood up. She could hear the pants of her own breathing, ragged against the melodious tones of the concerto, as she watched him strip off his shirt and kick off his shoes. He reached for his belt and suddenly sanity came flooding back.

What was she doing? What was she letting him do? She wasn't his mistress. Maybe she wasn't going to be able to resist him for long, but she would not be treated like some convenient sex toy—at his beck and call whenever he felt like it.

'Stop it. We're not making love,' she said, but the words came out on a barely audible croak.

He glanced up, his hands stilling on his belt. 'What was that, now?'

She shivered under the intensity of his gaze as he stared at her, sure she was about to catch fire. 'We're not making love until we've got a few things sorted out,' she said, her arms clasped so tightly around her breasts she could hardly breathe.

'What things?' he said, sounding mildly interested.

She gulped, spotting the impressive erection tenting the loose pleats in the front of his trousers. The muscles in her thighs went liquid and her sex throbbed painfully, an instinctive reaction to the memory of how good he'd once felt inside her. It seemed absence had only made her more of a nymphomaniac.

'I'm not your mistress. You may think I'm bought and paid

for. But I'm not.' She babbled to a stop. He was looking at her as if she'd taken leave of her senses. 'You don't own me,' she soldiered on regardless. 'And I won't be treated as if you do.'

He shrugged. 'Right enough,' he said, then pulled down his zipper. The crackle of the metal teeth unlocking drew her gaze down. 'Move over. I've a mind to join you in the tub.'

'I most certainly will…' But her indignant reply backed up in her throat as his trousers and boxers dropped to the floor and her eyes fixed on his groin. Unfortunately, he hadn't got any less beautiful, any less magnificent than the last time she'd seen him naked. Her whole body began to shake.

She gulped, her mouth bone-dry, and forced her eyes back to his face as he stepped into the tub. The sensual smile made it obvious he was very well aware of the effect his nakedness had on her.

He settled beside her, his big body making the water and her temperature rise. 'Now, where were we?' he said.

She lay transfixed by her raging hormones as he reached behind him for the soap.

She opened her mouth but no coherent sound came out as he lathered the soap then, nudging her arms to the side, placed his hands on her breasts. Her breath gushed out, sensation overwhelming her as he lifted the heavy orbs, his thumbs teasing swollen nipples. She arched up, closed her eyes, and groaned. Those demanding, purposeful fingers felt so good. She wanted him to touch her all over, everywhere. Her eyes jerked open, heat spiralling down to her core, when he captured her nipples and tugged.

'This is such a bad idea,' she whispered, swaying towards him and gripping his lean waist for balance as he continued to concentrate all his attention on her breasts.

He laughed, a raw, dominant chuckle that told her he knew exactly how good an idea her body thought it was. 'I know,' he rasped as she felt his erection nudge her thigh. 'I left the damn condoms in the other room.'

She flattened one hand on his chest, felt the silky resilience of smooth flesh over bunched muscles and tried to find the will to stop him. But then his palm glided down her abdomen and found the swollen flesh of her sex under the water.

His fingers explored, brushing her clitoris with the tiniest of touches and she bucked against him, crying out. He sealed off her cries with a harsh, demanding kiss, dragging her against him with one arm as his other hand continued to play havoc, stroking and caressing, pressing her sweet spot and then retreating. Her hips moved in a siren's rhythm, her fingers clutching at the back of his neck. He fastened his lips on the pulse in her throat, suckled as she threw her head back and gave herself up to the sensations exploding up from her core, only dimly aware of the water soaking the floor.

The orgasm roared through her, each wave pulsing over her body with greater intensity. The broken sobs of her release echoed as she collapsed against him, limp and shuddering, his embrace the only thing that was keeping her from sinking into the bath water and drowning.

She felt the insistent outline of his erection against her hip as his breath whispered across her ear lobe. 'Let's finish this in bed.' The words had barely registered when he stood up, hefted her in his arms and stepped out of the tub, splashing water everywhere.

'Put me down.' She struggled, the serene moment of after-glow wiped out by acute embarrassment.

Why had she let him march in and take over like that? Why had she succumbed so easily? She was more at his mercy now than ever.

He set her on her feet and threw her a towel before grabbing one for himself. She wrapped it around herself. The drenched bathmat squelched beneath her feet and the remnants of his suit lay sodden on the marble tiles. 'Look what you've done,' she cried, knowing she wasn't talking about the mess.

He smiled, rubbing the towel across his chest, the relaxed

grin casting a seductive spell. 'Don't worry, I intend to do a lot more—and soon.'

Heat scorched her insides as she realised just how far out of control things had become. He threw his towel away, then covered the fists she had anchored on hers with one large palm. 'Let go, angel. You don't need it.'

'I'm cold,' she murmured as she trembled, but she knew she wasn't.

'You won't be for long,' he said. Her fingers released of their own accord and he dragged the towel away. Lifting her against his chest, he carried her into the bedroom.

Her mind struggled to fight the sensual lethargy as he tumbled them onto the bed, trapping her beneath his body. She could feel every single inch of him, all firm muscle and lean masculine strength. She flattened her palms against his chest. 'Don't. I don't want you.' Her body screamed 'liar' as her mind struggled with the feeling of powerlessness, of being under his control.

He stiffened and something flashed in his eyes. 'I think you do,' he said, his voice strained. He took a condom from the dresser.

'You can't make me.' Her voice rose as she watched him sheath himself with single-minded efficiency.

'Make you?' He raised his head, one eyebrow bobbing up as his hand swept into her hair, cradled her head. 'I would never make you,' he said carefully, his thumb brushing her bottom lip. 'You must know that. But you're lying to yourself as well as me if you say you don't want me, angel.'

Strong hands gripped her thighs, angling her pelvis. 'Tell me again you don't want me and I'll let you go. I'll not force you,' he said.

She could feel the heat pulsing at her core, her chest heaving with longing, and knew she couldn't lie a second time. Couldn't bring herself to say the words that would deny her the pleasure he would give her.

The huge head of his erection probed. The pressure was immense as the slick folds of her sex tightened around him, but then he stopped.

The yearning to feel that one strong thrust that would force him deep, impale her, consumed her. But he didn't penetrate any further, the sinews in his neck taut as his eyes locked on hers.

'Ladies' choice, angel,' he murmured. His lips touched hers in a mocking kiss, tension vibrating through him. 'Now you tell me what it is you *do* want.'

Her hips flexed instinctively, and the delicious heat speared through her as he sank a fraction deeper. His fingers tightened, holding her still. She bit hard into her bottom lip, trapped and tortured by her own desires. Her own weakness.

'I want to hear you say it,' he said.

Her whole body clamoured for the release, for the blessed joy that only he had ever given her—and he knew it, she realised. She groaned, desperate to force the yearning back. Why was he making her beg? Hadn't she admitted enough? Hadn't she given him enough power? If she begged him now she'd be no better than a mistress—and maybe a great deal worse.

'Tell me you want me,' he demanded, his raw pants matching her own.

A staggered moan of surrender escaped her lips. 'Please… Do it. I want you. You know I do…'

A sharp dart of shame pierced her heart, but her mind disengaged as he thrust fully into her at last. He drove in up to the hilt, spearing through the tight, tender flesh and hurtling her over the edge. The orgasm burst free so much faster and stronger than before. She cried out, clutching his shoulders, clinging on as her legs locked around his waist. He pumped in and out in a furious, frenzied rhythm, filling her with an intensity, a ruthlessness that dragged her back with alarming speed and forced her over again—and again.

Finally, as she shattered into a million tiny glittering pieces, drained and exhausted from the relentless waves racking her body, he shouted out his own release—and shattered too.

CHAPTER ELEVEN

CONNOR collapsed onto his back, flung his arm across his face and struggled to draw a steady breath as his heartbeat battered his chest like a heavyweight champ's punching ball.

Where the hell had that come from?

One minute he'd been teasing her, enjoying the way her eyes darkened with desire, and the next he'd been gripped by a possessiveness, an intensity he didn't understand.

His affairs with women were always casual and fleeting. Sex was fun, fulfilling and must never be taken too seriously. He didn't do intense. So why had he turned into such a caveman when she'd told him she didn't want him?

The minute she'd said the words, he'd known she was lying. He'd seen the desire in her eyes, known all he had to do was touch her and she'd respond. But even so, he should have backed off, left well enough alone. Instead, something had welled up inside him, a bitterness, a resentment, a feeling of inadequacy he recognised from his childhood—and he'd been overwhelmed by the need to prove her wrong, to make her admit the truth.

He glanced across at her. She'd curled away from him, her shoulders trembling. He rose up on his elbow. Hell, was she crying? His heart clutched in his chest.

He pulled the quilt up to cover them both, smoothed his hand over her hip. She shifted away.

'Daisy, are you all right?'

'Of course,' she said, but her voice sounded small and fragile. He studied the sprinkling of freckles across her shoulder
blades, the way her damp hair was already springing up
around her head. She looked so delicate to him all of a sudden.
He winced. She'd been so tight around him and yet he'd taken
her like a man possessed. Had he hurt her?

'Are you sure?' he asked, not sure he wanted to hear the
answer.

She didn't reply, just sat up with her back to him, and
pulled the thin cotton shift she'd left beside the bed over her
head. He watched her movements, jerky and tense. The urge
to hold her, to comfort her, to make up for what he'd done,
blindsided him.

He stiffened. What the hell was happening to him? He
didn't even recognise himself. She'd done something to him.
Come to mean something he didn't understand.

In the last week he hadn't been able to stop thinking about
her. Getting her to New York had been a game—a way of
showing her the error of her ways, and enjoying some great
recreational sex into the bargain. Or so he'd tried to tell himself.

But if it was all a game, why had he bought her a ten-
thousand-euro necklace without a thought when he'd been
window-shopping in the Marais? Sure he was usually generous
with the women he dated, but not that generous after only one
date. Why had he spent over an hour outlining his plans for her
trip with his PA? Why had he called the airline first thing that
morning to check she'd boarded the flight? And why had he
cancelled the rest of his meetings and raced back to The
Waldorf as soon as he'd got the word she'd checked in?

He'd been behaving like an over-eager puppy begging for
scraps. It made him feel vulnerable in a way he hadn't since
he was a lad. But he hadn't been able to stop himself.

And then, to make matters worse, when he'd walked into
the bathroom and seen her lush body covered in soap suds,

her soft flesh pink from the heat, the expected sexual charge had been swiftly followed by a blast of euphoria and bone-deep satisfaction that made no sense at all.

Given all that, was it any surprise that when she'd told him she wanted no part of him he'd been bound and determined to prove her a liar? To prove that she did want him—because he wanted her so damn much it was starting to scare him.

'Daisy, will you look at me?' he said, his patience stretching. 'I want to see you're okay.'

She glanced over her shoulder.

Relief washed through him when he saw no evidence of tears.

'Why wouldn't I be okay?' Green fire flashed as she faced him. 'You gave me what I wanted, right? What you made me beg for. You should be pretty pleased with yourself, all things considered.'

An unreasoning panic seized him as she turned away and he leaped forward to catch her arm.

'Wait.' His fingers clamped on her wrist.

Whatever had happened, they'd have to sort it out, because he wasn't ready to let her walk—not yet. Not until he sorted out what the hell was happening to him. She'd triggered something inside him and he needed her here to make it stop.

'Let go of me,' she said, her head bowed as she tried to wrestle her hand free. 'I'm not staying. You'll have to find another fake date. The sex is great, but the subservience I can do without, thank you.'

He dropped his feet on the floor, sat on the edge of the bed and pulled her to him when she tried to resist. 'Daisy, I'm sorry.'

He'd never apologised to any woman before her—he'd never needed to—and the words burned like acid on his tongue. He figured they'd been worth it, though, when she stopped struggling and looked at him. Anger still simmered, but behind it was something much harder to fathom.

'What are you apologising for?' she asked, her voice flat and remote. 'For giving me my first multiple orgasm?'

He had hurt her. He could see now he'd humiliated her. He knew a lot about pride and what it felt like to have it beaten out of you. Enough to know how much it hurt.

He took her other wrist and tugged her towards him, pressing his knees into her thighs, to keep her near. 'It wasn't meant as a punishment,' he said. He rested his hands on her hips, blew out a breath as he touched his cheek to the soft cotton covering her breasts. Her hands remained limply by her side, the muscles of her spine rigid beneath his fingers as she arched away from him. Lavender, underlaid with the scent of her, made blood surge into his groin, he hoped to hell she couldn't see it beneath the thick folds of the quilt. He raised his head, saw the flush of unhappiness and something else he didn't recognise on her face.

'Why did you make me beg for it, then?' she asked, accusation weighing every word. 'It was cruel and humiliating. What were you trying to prove?' Her frankness and vulnerability stunned him—and made him feel like a worm.

He shrugged, keeping his hands on her waist so she couldn't pull back any further.

'I wanted you to stay. And it seemed like a good way to persuade you.'

It wasn't the whole truth. In fact it wasn't even half of the truth. But he could hardly tell her how desperate he'd been to see her, how much he'd been looking forward to her coming over. It would make him look like a besotted idiot—and give her entirely the wrong impression.

Women always tried to romanticise sex—especially exceptional sex. And that was all this was really about. No woman had ever responded to him as she did, no woman had ever affected him quite like her before. But once he got her out of his system things would be fine.

Obviously his desire to stamp his claim on her had been brought on by sexual frustration. He'd never been this attracted to a woman in his life. But that would pass soon enough, he was sure of it. Romance had no part of it. Not for him.

'Why did you have to make me say it?' she asked, the words more confused than angry.

He choked out a half-laugh. Christ, why had he? 'I don't know.' And he was pretty sure now he didn't want to know. Best to leave that can of worms well enough alone. He'd just have to make damn sure he didn't lose his cool with her and open it up all over again.

Her eyes sharpened and he could see she didn't believe him. But then she sighed and her shoulders slumped. Finally she looked back at him and what he saw, to his amazement, was guilt.

'I know you paid a lot of money to get me here. And you didn't force me, not really. I wanted to come. I've never been to New York before.' She glanced round the room. 'And this place is incredible. But it's all so overwhelming. And I can't stay here as your mistress. It's demeaning.' Her brow furrowed. 'If you still need someone to pose as your girlfriend you can get me a cheap room, somewhere else, and I'll still do it. Then you won't be out of pocket. Okay?'

His heart contracted at the seriousness on her face. Damn. He'd known she was a Good Samaritan but this was stupid. He couldn't care less about her 'posing' as his girlfriend or the money he'd spent getting her here. Truth was he'd been showing off a little, wanting to dazzle her, trying to make sure she came. Who would have known his attempts to impress her would backfire?

He sighed. He should have guessed she'd be the first woman to be turned off by the money instead of turned on by it. She was so contrary.

But how could he tell her how much he wanted her with him and not make it sound as if there were more going on than there actually was? He needed to lighten the mood, get things back on their proper footing, not make them more intense.

Then a vague recollection of what Danny had said about the whole Melrose problem came to him and he had his answer in a flash of divine inspiration.

'You'll stay here with me, Daisy. You didn't just come for New York or The Waldorf. You came because you want me and I want you. And after what just happened there'll be no more denying it.' That at least he intended to make very plain.

She stiffened. 'I don't care. I told you I won't be your—'

'Shush now,' he said, feeling the flutter of her pulse as he pressed his thumb into her wrist. 'I've a solution to the problem that should satisfy your pride.'

He gave her a friendly pat on the rump. 'Go get some clothes on. We've a lot to do before we can have supper and I'm famished.'

Instructing her to meet him in the lobby in twenty minutes, Connor left Daisy to get dressed in the private dressing room. As she prepared herself for the evening ahead Daisy got the distinct impression she'd just been railroaded, but she felt too bewildered to worry about it now. She needed some time alone, to make sense of what had happened. Of what she'd let happen.

She'd been so angry and humiliated after they'd made love—correction: after she'd begged him to make love to her, again—that she'd wanted to hate him.

But then he'd apologised, and she'd been forced to face the truth. He'd been honest about how much he wanted her and she hadn't. And then she'd been doubly humiliated. Not only could she not resist him, but she couldn't even claim the moral high ground now either.

As she dabbed on make-up and slipped into the vintage satin halter-neck dress she'd made she admitted that her protests that afternoon had made her seem like the worst kind of hypocritical prude. Had she really pretended to herself when she'd got on that plane—with a dazzling array of hooker underwear in her suitcase and the memory of their last sexual encounter still vivid in her mind—that she wasn't going to sleep with him?

She'd been deluding herself all along and all he'd done was point it out to her—in a rather forceful manner. The fairy-tale fantasy that had lured her onto the plane didn't just involve the glitz and glamour of a luxury fortnight in New York. She'd also been enthralled by Connor Brody and the incredible sexual chemistry they shared.

She stepped out of the penthouse lift, her pulse skittering as she saw Connor walking towards her, looking devastating in another of his designer suits. She wanted him, more than she'd ever wanted any man, and, however disturbing that might be to her peace of mind, she would have to stop denying it if she was going to learn to handle it.

Connor ushered her into the limo, and the small of her back sizzled under the warm weight of his palm. She sat back as the car sped off, watched the dizzying sights and sounds of Park Avenue roll by, and attempted to revise her survival strategy. Okay, staying out of Connor's bed was not going to be a viable option for the next two weeks. But her basic theory was still sound. All she had to do was make sure she didn't let her heart follow her hormones.

She watched as Connor leaned forward to give the driver instructions. Jet-black hair curled against the light-blue collar of his shirt; she clasped the purse in her lap and resisted the urge to run her fingers through the silky locks. Connor Brody was a dangerous man: dangerously attractive, dangerously desirable and dangerously single-minded. When he wanted something he went after it. And at the moment he wanted her.

She gazed back out of the window, tearing her eyes away from him.

But he'd already told her this was strictly a two-week deal—and that suited her too. She wasn't going to start looking for her happy ever after with a guy who wasn't remotely interested. She wasn't her mother and this was her chance to prove it once and for all.

After their two weeks were up she would make sure she

walked away from this relationship with some enchanting memories to savour and her heart one hundred per cent whole. The next fortnight would be a grand adventure that she intended to make the absolute most of, but it was not real life.

'We're here,' Connor said, taking her hand and stepping onto the sidewalk.

Daisy stared at the iconic jewellery stall as he tipped the driver. 'What are we doing here?'

'It's all part of the solution to our problem.' He cupped her elbow in his palm. 'By the way,' he said, his eyes sweeping her frame, 'that dress is deadly.'

Although the compliment pleased her, probably more than it should, she ignored the little leap in her pulse rate. He was railroading her again. And it was about time she put the brakes on. He'd called enough of the shots already.

'What solution?' she asked as he pushed the revolving door and stepped in behind her.

He settled his hand on the nape of her neck, his thumb stroking the sensitive skin. 'I'm buying you an engagement ring.'

And just like that, her senses went haywire and her calm, measured, practical approach to the whole situation went up in flames.

'I'm not wearing it. This is ridiculous.' She tried to tug her hand out of his grasp, but he simply lifted her fist and brushed his lips across the knuckles.

'Stop sulking, angel.' He sent her a teasing smile. 'Maureen will think you don't like the ring.' He nodded towards the sales lady, who was pretending to stack some of the store's signature blue and silver boxes.

'It's not that and you know it,' she snapped, hoping Maureen couldn't hear them. 'I can't wear it.'

Having endured the ten-minute charade as he and Maureen had ummed and ahhed over a selection of engagement rings until he'd finally picked out a delicate silver band studded with diamonds, Daisy wasn't sulking, she was in a state of shock.

She didn't want to wear the heartbreakingly beautiful ring.

She'd once dreamt of the moment when a man she loved and who loved her in return would put an engagement ring on her finger. Connor wasn't that man, would never be that man and this definitely wasn't that moment. She knew that. But she still didn't want him to put that ring on her finger.

'Why can't you wear it?' he asked, flattening her hand between his palms, turning it over. 'You don't want to be my mistress. Fine, I understand that. So we put the ring on. You become my fiancée for the next two weeks. Problem solved.'

She looked at him, saw the confidence, the arrogance and that devilish determination and wanted to kick him—not to mention herself. How could she explain her objections without coming across as a romantic fool? And why had she objected to being his mistress in the first place? When the alternative he'd found seemed a thousand times more disturbing. She felt as if she'd sashayed out of the frying pan and crashed headlong into the fire.

'But I'm not your fiancée. It would be a lie. I don't think it's right. To lie, that is.' Great, now she sounded like a self-righteous prig instead.

He chuckled. 'Angel, don't take this so seriously. It's only for two weeks.' He brushed her cheek. 'We have some fun, my business deal is settled and no one's pride is compromised. Fair enough?'

It sounded so reasonable when he said it like that. Was she blowing this out of proportion? Making a big deal about nothing? Hadn't Mrs Valdermeyer also accused her of taking things too seriously? If she wanted to enjoy the next two weeks, make the most of them, didn't she have to learn to relax first?

She sighed. 'Fine, but you'll have to do all the introductions. I'm not good at lying to people.'

He smiled. 'It won't be a lie, just one of the shortest en-gagements on record,' he said and slipped the ring on her finger. But as the cool silver slid down she felt another band tighten around her heart.

Connor felt the slight tremble as he held her wrist to push the ring home. He steadfastly ignored the answering jump in his pulse. Sure he'd never put a ring on any woman's finger before, and never intended to again. The strange surge of pride, of satisfaction as he did it, didn't mean a thing. Not a blessed thing.

CHAPTER TWELVE

'I'VE got to tell you, it's been fabulous meeting you, Daisy,' Jessie Latimer said, her bright face brimming with enthusiasm. 'Monroe and I always knew the woman to capture Connor's heart would have to be very special. After all, he's quite a handful.'

'Yes, he is.' Daisy clutched the stem of her champagne glass and forced herself to smile back—not easy when her face ached and she felt as if she were about to throw up. Connor Brody wasn't just a handful, he was quite possibly a dead man after putting her in this excruciating predicament. Especially as it had come totally out of the blue.

The last week had gone by in a whirlwind of sights, sounds and activities. Daisy had never been anywhere as full on as New York before or with anyone as full on as Connor. And, despite all her misgivings, they'd had a wonderful time. They'd managed to pack in the Metropolitan Opera, the Met, Coney Island and the Circle Line tour, and in between times had had the best sex of Daisy's life. Because Connor was as full on a lover as he was a tour guide, but she'd soaked up every amazing sight and mind-blowing sexual experience and found she still wanted more. They'd both been determined to keep things light and non-committal. They didn't talk about the future and they didn't delve into each other's real lives and, as a consequence, she'd had very little time to dwell on the whole 'fake engagement' thing.

She thought she'd been handling it really well.

In fact, in the last six days, she'd only had two major hurdles to overcome. The worst had been the first night, when she'd tried to take the ring off in the bathroom of their suite and Connor had asked her to leave it on. He'd given her some excuse about not wanting to buy another if she lost it, a cocky smile on his lips, but when they'd made love that night and she'd spotted the ring winking at her she'd felt that funny clutch in her heart again. And it had taken her over an hour to fall asleep, despite the jet lag.

She'd handled the second hurdle much better. Being introduced to a group of Connor's business associates at an exclusive cocktail party the previous night had been a cinch in comparison. She'd decided that she'd settled into the charade now and it would be plain sailing from here on in. All she need do was think of herself as an actress playing a role.

But then they'd arrived at the opening of the brand-new Latimer Gallery twenty minutes ago, and Connor had introduced her to Monroe Latimer—a world-famous artist whose work Daisy had admired at the Tate Britain only a few months ago—and his wife, Jessie. And the subterfuge of pretending to be Connor's fiancée had become a thousand times tougher.

It had been obvious as soon as they'd been introduced that the couple were close friends of Connor. As he'd given her no warning, Daisy had assumed that Connor would simply tell them the truth. But when Jessie had spotted the ring and got excited, Connor had lied without a qualm, even talking about their wedding plans, before Monroe had dragged him off to find a beer.

Consequently, Daisy had been stuck lying through her teeth to a woman she'd warmed to instantly. A fellow Brit, Jessie Latimer had been friendly and funny and welcoming from the get-go; she'd been gracious and not at all big-headed when Daisy had gushed about the gallery and her husband's work and told Daisy some sweet and charming anecdotes about the couple's three daughters and what it was like to be an Englishwoman in New York. But the instant they'd got onto the subject of Daisy's impending nuptials, Daisy had felt as if she were being strangled by her conscience.

She wasn't a dishonest person—and she was fast discovering that she was a rubbish actress too.

'You're so different from the other women he's dated,' Jessie said. Her eyes widened and she touched Daisy's arm. 'God, I'm sorry, that sounded really gauche. But I mean it in the best possible way. Monroe and I have known him for three years now—ever since we started this project.' She glanced round the loft-style space in Tribeca which housed some of New York's most prestigious modern art. 'We hit it off with Connor right away, not just as an investment partner but as a friend,' Jessie continued. 'But Monroe and I could never get over some of the bimbos he dated.' She gave an easy laugh. 'I'm so glad he's finally found a woman who can match him. It's what he's always needed in his life, I suspect. Although it's taken him a hell of a long time to figure it out.'

Daisy felt her fake smile crack. Why had he lied to his friends like this? It was awful. The diamond ring felt like a lead weight on her finger as she lifted the champagne flute to her lips and took a fortifying sip. Her heart pounded so hard in her throat it threatened to cut off her air supply.

'Is there something wrong, Daisy? You're looking a little pale.'

Daisy's stomach took a swooping drop. This was the moment of truth. She couldn't continue lying to this woman. No wonder she looked pale—she was definitely going to be sick any moment.

'I don't know how to say this,' she said, her fingers shaking on the glass and making the champagne slop to the rim.

'What is it?' Concern darkened Jessie's eyes, making Daisy feel like even more of a fraud.

'We're not engaged. Connor and I.'

Jessie's eyebrows shot up. 'You're not?'

'No.' Daisy stared down at her hands, the glint of diamonds on her ring finger only adding to her shame. 'We're not getting married. We only met two weeks ago. He's my neighbour. He paid for me to come here so I could pose as his fiancée.'

God, the whole thing sounded so unbearably sordid. She looked up, steeling herself to deal with the disgust she expected to see on Jessie's face.

But she didn't see disgust. Jessie's shoulders trembled and then, to Daisy's complete astonishment, she started to laugh.

'You're kidding?' Jessie blurted out at last, when she could finally draw a steady breath.

Daisy shrugged, acutely embarrassed. 'No, I'm not. It's dreadful, I know. He's deceived you and Monroe. I've deceived you…' She trailed off, not sure what else to say when Jessie had to clasp her hand over her mouth to hold back her giggling fit.

As she stood there, listening to Jessie's muffled laughter and watching the beautiful people nearby craning their necks to stare at them, Daisy began to wonder what was worse—being Connor Brody's scarlet woman or a complete laughing stock.

'I'm so sorry. Don't be embarrassed.' Jessie squeezed her arm, managing to subdue her mirth with an effort. 'It's just, you have no idea how ironic this is.'

'Thanks for taking it so well,' she said tentatively.

'Don't mention it,' Jessie said, still grinning. 'Look, I hope you don't mind me asking this. But it's obvious you're not comfortable with this whole set-up. Why did you agree to do it?'

Daisy blew out a breath. 'That's a good question. And it's sort of complicated.'

'I'm sure it is,' Jessie said. 'And I don't mean to pry. But Connor's a good friend, and I'd love to know what's going on between the two of you.'

'It might take a while to explain it, from my point of view anyway,' Daisy said, realising to her surprise she didn't mind giving Jessie her answer. After all, she'd given the question a lot of thought over the last week and it was about time she came clean about her motives—to herself as well as Jessie.

'Honey.' Jessie smiled. 'We've got all evening, or at least until Monroe and Connor find a beer, which could take a while seeing as the caterers only stocked champagne for this event as far as I know.'

'All right,' Daisy said, taking a deep breath. 'First off, I should tell you I live in a bedsit in West London. I work six days a week on my stall in Portobello Market. And this whole scene…' she did a circling motion with her glass to encompass the glittering crowd of Manhattan's movers and shakers surrounding them '…is about as far from my real life as it's possible to get. I help out at the local old people's home once a week. I run the Carnival Arts project for the kids on a nearby council estate. I mentor and volunteer and I'm totally committed to my friends and my community.'

'Now I know why I liked you instantly,' Jessie said easily.

Bolstered by the appreciation she saw in Jessie's face, Daisy smiled. 'Don't get me wrong. I love my life. I love the stability and the purpose and the sense of belonging it gives me and I intend to build on that when I have my own family one day. And I'm not interested in becoming rich or anything.' She hesitated for a moment, stroked the stem of her glass. 'But I've spent my whole life being cautious, and practical and responsible until I find my Mr Right.' She looked at Jessie, saw the compassion in her eyes, but decided against bringing up her mother's misbegotten love life—that seemed a bit too personal. 'Connor, like the world he lives in, is the complete antithesis of my Mr Right. He's exciting, sexy, charming, completely spontaneous and totally unreliable.'

And the best lover I've ever had, she thought, but decided not to mention that either. After all, she didn't want Jessie to think she was a total slut.

'He's the opposite of what I'm looking for in a life partner.

He's not dependable or interested in settling down and I totally understand that. So I'm not under any delusions.' Thank goodness. 'But right here, right now, I guess he's a guilty pleasure that I couldn't resist. I decided when I got his plane ticket, these two weeks were going to be my Cinderella fortnight and so far they've worked out really well.' Give or take the odd heart bump. 'But once this is over I'll be happy to go back to my real life and my real dreams.'

'I see,' Jessie said, giving her a considering look.

'I guess that sounds as if I'm using him,' Daisy said quickly, realising how it sounded now she'd spelled it out so succinctly. She started to feel a little queasy again. This woman was Connor's friend, after all, not hers, however much she might want her to be. 'But as he's using me right back,' she continued, 'I don't feel guilty about it.' Or she was trying hard not to.

'I don't think you're using him,' Jessie said staunchly.

'You don't?' The knots in Daisy's stomach loosened.

'No, I don't,' Jessie said firmly. 'And even if you were, it would serve him right.' She sent Daisy a quick grin. 'The words *hoisted* and *petard* springing to mind.'

Daisy's breath gushed out in a relieved huff. Maybe Jessie's approval shouldn't mean so much to her, but somehow it did.

'But I've got to tell you,' Jessie continued, 'I do think you might be selling Connor a little short. At least as far as you're concerned.'

Daisy's heartbeat kicked hard in her chest, her breathing becoming uneven again. She wasn't sure she liked the wistful look in Jessie's eyes. 'How so?'

Jessie stared at her for a long moment. 'The Connor you described—the handsome, reckless, unreliable charmer—is only the Connor you see on the surface. That's the face he shows to the world and that's the way he likes everyone to see him. Especially women.'

Jessie paused to pick up a canapé from the tray of a passing waiter, but her eyes barely left Daisy's. 'It's the way he came across to Monroe and I when we first met him.' Jessie bit into the salmon puff, took her time swallowing it. 'In fact when we got involved with this project we were both worried about him. He'd come recommended, but still we thought, Can we count on him? Will he bail out if the going gets tough? We were putting a lot of money on the line and as much as we liked him personally we weren't sure about him. Precisely because he seemed so relaxed, so easy-going, almost overconfident.'

'So why did you risk it?' Daisy asked, intrigued despite herself. She'd never asked Connor about his work, just as he'd never asked her about her stall. It was all part of that unwritten agreement they had that this wasn't a serious relationship, but, still, she wanted to know more.

'Originally we went ahead because I got my brother-in-law Linc, who's a Wall Street financier, to do a thorough check on Brody Construction. The company's still young, even now, but it came out with flying colours, so we signed the partnership deal with Connor.' Jessie huffed. 'Almost straight away things started to go wrong on the project. The permits took much longer to come through than originally forecast. One of the suppliers went into receivership out of the blue. The building had a structural problem that hadn't come up on the survey. Talk about a money pit. Frankly, the whole rehab was a complete nightmare.' She grinned. 'Connor, though, turned out to be our knight in shining armour, and the exact opposite of what he had first seemed. He was dedicated, conscientious, incredibly hard-working, inventive and one hundred and ten per cent reliable. He even put on a tool belt himself a couple of times towards the end of the build to get things done.'

Daisy felt her chest swell with pride at Jessie's praise—and then felt ridiculous. After all Connor wasn't even her proper boyfriend. She began to wonder if she really needed to know about this side of him. It had been so much easier to dismiss him as a feckless charmer.

'It's nice to know he's so good at his job,' she said, trying hard to sound non-committal. 'He must enjoy it, which is probably why he's so successful.'

'He does enjoy it. But I'd say what he enjoys most is the challenge. Which brings us to the fascinating subject of Connor's love life. Which has never been remotely challenging.'

Daisy sipped her champagne, but the bubbles did nothing to ease the dryness in her throat. She really didn't need to know about his past relationships with women. Especially as their relationship had a sell-by date that was fast approaching. Now would be a good time to change the subject.

'What were they like?' she asked. 'The other women he's dated?' Blast, where had that come from?

'Interchangeable and shallow,' Jessie said, before Daisy could take the question back. 'I was being a bit unfair calling them bimbos, though. Some of them have been very shrewd. The last one he dated, Rachel, being a case in point. I wasn't at all surprised when she told Connor she was pregnant.'

Daisy bobbled her glass. 'Connor has a child?'

'Of course not,' Jessie said. 'She wasn't pregnant. It was what you might call a very convenient scare. Just when he was trying to end the relationship.'

'What did he do?' Daisy asked, riveted by the topic despite everything.

'To everyone's astonishment he offered to marry her, to support the child. Even though Monroe and I both knew it was the last thing he wanted to do. When he told us she wasn't pregnant after all, he looked like a guy who had escaped the executioner's block.'

'He didn't want to be a father?' Daisy said, feeling strangely depressed, even though she already knew Connor wasn't the family man type.

'I don't think it's quite that simple. I don't know for sure, but I think he had a really tough childhood and his attitude to kids and family is very confused because of it. But one thing I do know is that he is petrified of commitment. He's a property developer but as far as I know the place he's rehabbed in London, the house next door to yours, is the first home he's ever bought for himself.'

'I see,' Daisy said, feeling even more dispirited.

Jessie sent her a knowing smile. 'Which makes it all the more bizarre that he's put his ring on your finger less than two weeks after meeting you.'

Daisy glanced at the ring, which seemed to have got even heavier while they were talking. 'Yes, but I've told you it's not a real commitment. On his part or mine.'

'Are you sure?' Jessie cut her off.

Daisy blinked. Swallowed. Of course she was sure, because anything else didn't bear thinking about. But somehow the denial got lodged in Daisy's throat.

'There are several things about this situation that don't add up, Daisy,' Jessie continued. 'First off, it's very noticeable how different you are from the other women Connor's dated. You're not shallow, or stupid, or shrewd. Second off, he treats you differently from the way he treated them. I mean, he walked in here with you on his arm and basically staked you out as his for everyone to see. He's never done that before. He's not the possessive type. Not till now anyway.' Jessie took Daisy's hand and held up the ring. 'And this whole fake engagement thing. It seems a bit extreme. Why does someone like Connor need a fake fiancée? That I'd really like to know.'

'He hasn't said, not specifically,' Daisy replied, and decided then and there she was never going to ask him. Because everything Jessie was saying was making her feel very uneasy.

'Fine,' Jessie said. 'But I guess what I'm really saying is, I know Connor. And I think there's a lot more going on here than either he or you realise.'

Daisy gulped in a breath, felt her heart pound against her

chest wall like a battering ram. Now she really couldn't breathe. This she definitely did not want to hear. Because she could see a great big chasm opening up at her feet.

One she had no intention of jumping into.

She pulled her hand out of Jessie's grasp. 'I'm really flattered that you'd think I'm special, or different,' she said carefully, 'but I'm not.'

'To which I'd have to say,' Jessie countered, 'that if you really think that, you're selling yourself short, as well as Connor.'

Daisy lifted her glass of champagne, ignored the way it trembled as she took a sip.

She couldn't do this. She couldn't afford to think for even a moment that this thing with Connor could be anything more than it was, because that way lay serious danger. She couldn't afford to fall in love with a man who was petrified of commitment, for whatever reason. And she didn't want to.

Jessie, she decided, was just a hopeless romantic, who clearly cared deeply about Connor and wanted him to be happy. But whatever Jessie might think about their so-called relationship, it wouldn't change the outcome of their two-week fling. And Daisy was far too practical and well grounded to think it could.

'There's no big romance here, Jessie,' she said, but her voice wasn't quite as firm as it should be.

Jessie simply smiled and said, 'Don't be so sure.'

'Right, spill it, buddy, what's between you and that cute little redhead?' Monroe Latimer slanted Connor his 'you're busted' look and slugged back the last of his beer. 'And don't tell me she's your fiancée.' He dropped the empty bottle onto the bar. 'You may have got Red fooled, but I happen to know wild horses couldn't get you to propose.'

'Fair enough.' Connor lifted his hands in surrender, knowing when he'd been rumbled. He'd planned to tell Monroe the truth straight away, but, well, what with one thing and another, they'd been at the bar for twenty minutes partaking of Monroe's secret stash of beer and he hadn't quite got round to it. 'She's not my fiancée. She's my new neighbour in London. She's smart and pretty and, for reasons too boring to mention…' and way too transparent to mention to Monroe '…I needed a girlfriend while I was here and she fitted the bill. No strings attached.'

'Hmm,' Monroe said, keeping his eyes on Connor as he signalled the barman for a fresh beer. 'Which does *not* explain why you told Red and me she was your fiancée. Or why you bought her what has to be a real pricey ring.'

Connor took a gulp of his own beer. 'It's complicated.'

'I'll bet,' Monroe said, looking at him as if he were a bug under a microscope.

'And not the least bit interesting,' he countered.

'Humour me.'

Connor gave a half-laugh, although he wasn't finding being a bug all that amusing any more.

Monroe was a mate, a good mate. They'd even got drunk together one night and told each other more about their pasts than either of them was comfortable with—and their friendship had survived it. But there was one thing they'd never agreed on. And that was the subject of love and family.

That same night, when they'd been legless and overly sentimental, Connor had told Monroe that he would never fall in love. And Monroe had told him right back that he was talking a load of bull. Monroe had said that a guy didn't get to pick and choose those things, which Connor had thought then, and still thought now, was even bigger bull. Maybe Monroe had been blindsided and fallen in love with Jessie, and once Connor had got to know Jessie he could see why, but Connor knew that would never, ever happen to him.

Because what Monroe didn't know, what no one knew, was raising a family, having a home, was Connor's idea of hell. And no woman would ever be able to change that for him.

Christ, when Rachel had told him she was pregnant, his whole life had flashed before his eyes—and not in a good way.

He knew Monroe and Jessie thought his reaction had been down to the fact that Rachel wasn't the right woman for him, but he knew different. He knew it had nothing to do with the woman. It went much deeper than that, and much further back. He'd offered to marry her, to support the baby, because he couldn't live with himself and know a child of his had been left to fend for itself. But that hadn't changed his gut reaction. He didn't want the child and he didn't want a wife. Any wife. And he was fine with that, fine and dandy.

He could tell by the way his friend was looking at him right now, though, that Monroe thought this little charade with Daisy was somehow significant. Sure he'd enjoyed her company in the last week. He'd got a thrill out of showing her the sights, and seeing her wide-eyed, enthusiastic reaction to everything. And in bed? Let's just say she'd exceeded his wildest expectations. He'd even got an unexpected kick out of showing her off as his fiancée. But that was all there was to it. A week from now they'd go their separate ways and that would be that. So Connor intended to head his friend's misconception right off at the pass.

'All right,' he sighed. 'I should have been straight with you and Jessie. But after all the matchmaking advice I've had to endure from your lovely wife over the last three years, Roe. You've got to know, I couldn't resist when she spotted the ring.'

'Fair point.' Monroe saluted him with his bottle of beer. 'I'll grant you Jessie is pretty damn persistent. But I hope you realise your little joke is going to backfire on you.'

'She'll forgive me,' he said, feeling his confidence returning. He raised his eyebrows. 'After all, she can't resist my irresistible Irish charm.'

'Yeah, right.' Monroe laughed. 'But that's not what I meant.'

'What did you mean, then?' Why didn't he feel quite so confident any more?

'I gotta tell you, for a minute there you had me fooled as well as Jessie. You want to know why?'

Connor didn't say a word.

'Because you fit,' Monroe said, and Connor's heart stopped dead. 'You and your cute little redhead. Daisy, that's her name, right?'

Connor nodded dumbly, trying to pull himself together. This was ludicrous. Monroe was just trying to get a rise out of him. And it was working.

'She suits you, pal,' Monroe said, swigging his beer. 'Right down to the ground. I'm an artist, I happen to have an eye for these things and I'm telling you. She's the one.'

Connor growled a profanity under his breath, his stomach churning as he tried to see the joke. But why did it suddenly seem as if the joke was on him?

Monroe chuckled. 'Hey, what happened to that irresistible Irish charm, buddy?'

'Why didn't you tell me Jessie and Monroe were friends of yours before we got to the gallery tonight?' Daisy pulled out her earrings and dropped them in a bowl by the vanity.

She'd bided her time, not wanting to bring it up until she'd got a good firm grip on her own emotions. After the shock Jessie had given her it had taken a while.

'Hmm?' he said from behind her, then his hands settled on her waist. He pulled her into his arms, his naked chest warm against her back. 'You looked lovely tonight, you know,' he said, rubbing the silk of her slip against her belly as he nuzzled her ear. 'I may have to hire you for this gig again.'

The comment—and the heat drifting up from her sex at his casual caresses—couldn't have been calculated to ignite her temper quicker if he'd tried.

She turned in his arms, pushed against the muscled flesh. 'It's not funny,' she said, suddenly feeling more hurt than angry and hating herself for her weakness. 'You put me in a really difficult position. Not only not telling me you knew them, but then telling them we were getting married. And leaving me with Jessie like that. I felt awful. You knew I didn't want to lie to people. It wasn't fair.'

He stepped back, but kept his hands firmly on her waist. 'Come on, angel.' He tucked a finger under her chin, lifted her face to his. 'Don't look so upset. There was no harm done. They figured it out quick enough.'

'Jessie didn't. I had to tell her.' She turned away from him, braced her hands on the vanity.

And what Jessie had told her afterwards was still clutching at her heart, making panic clog her throat. Somehow her fantasy had changed tonight and become so much more real, and so much more frightening. She'd kept all the turbulent emotions at bay so effectively this past week, sealed herself off behind a wall of denial and sensation, but now the feel of his hands on hers, that clean, musky, masculine scent had become more intoxicating, more important to her than it was ever supposed to have been.

'I don't understand why you did that,' she said, raising her head to look at his reflection. With his shirt off and his chest bare, he looked as dark and devastating as always, but so much more dangerous now. 'Why did you introduce me to them as your fiancée?'

He shrugged. 'Just an impulse, I guess.' He had the lazy grin in place, but his eyes flickered away from hers as he said it. 'Stop worrying.' He pushed her hair back, trailed his thumb down the sensitive skin of her neck. 'Let's go to bed and forget it.' He pressed his lips to her pulse. 'I've got something much more interesting to discuss,' he whispered, one arm wrapping tight around her waist, his other hand cupping her breast, kneading the swollen flesh.

She moaned. His erection pressed against her bottom through their clothes, triggering the instant, instinctive response at her core. She angled her head to accept his harsh, demanding kiss, gave herself up to the heat, desperate to forget about everything but the feel of his body, the touch of his hands, his lips on hers.

He hadn't given her an answer. She knew that, but did she really want one?

She turned in his arms, encircled his neck with trembling hands, suddenly determined to cling onto the one thing that made sense.

'This is all that matters, angel,' he said, lifting her effortlessly in his arms and carrying her quaking into the bedroom. 'This is all that counts. Remember that.'

Yes. This is all that matters. I'm not looking for anything else.

But even as she threw herself into the moment, even as she chased that glittering oblivion, panic and an unreasonable regret gripped her heart.

CHAPTER THIRTEEN

As Daisy shielded her eyes to gaze at Belvedere Castle across the meadow, a bittersweet smile tugged her lips. With its fanciful turret and fortress ramparts, the elaborate folly could have been plucked straight out of a Grimm Brothers fairy tale and plopped into the middle of Central Park.

She sighed. No daydreaming allowed. It was their last full day in New York and somehow she'd managed to live in the moment in the last week, keep the doubts and uncertainties Jessie had unleashed at the gallery opening locked carefully away. She wasn't going to blow it all now.

The fact that Connor had turned out to be an expert at living in the moment hadn't hurt a bit. Whenever she'd found her mind drifting to more serious matters, whenever she'd found herself watching him and wondering, he'd found a way to distract her. With a ferry trip round the Statue of Liberty, or a deluxe dinner at his favourite restaurant, or in bed, where he had become an expert in making her forget everything but the heat between them.

But in the few quiet moments they shared, she had a bad habit of thinking about what might have been. If they'd been different people, if they'd needed the same things. She tried really hard not to let her thoughts go there, but right now, with the cartons from their impromptu picnic scattered around them and that damn fairy-tale castle looming on the other side of the meadow, she couldn't seem to stop herself.

After the Governor's Ball tonight and the first-class trip home tomorrow, she would be going back to her real life and, as much as she didn't want to admit it, she knew the thing she'd miss the most, much more than the glamour and the excitement, was the intimacy she'd shared with Connor. He'd be right next door, of course, but as far as she was concerned he'd be out of reach. She had to make a clean break, whatever happened; to let it drift on indefinitely would be suicidal and, anyway, they'd both known right from the start this was strictly a two-week deal.

The sun warmed the floppy hat she'd worn to hide her freckles as she observed Connor stretched out beside her in the long grass, his hands folded behind his head, and his eyes shaded by a pair of designer sunglasses. The hem of his T-shirt had risen up revealing a strip of tanned abdomen above the low waistband of his jeans.

She let her mind drift back to that first night, when she'd yearned to touch his naked body. She knew every glorious inch of it now—and she still had to fist her hands in her lap to stop herself from reaching out and running her palm over that warm, flat, lightly furred belly.

Well, that was certainly disappointing: two weeks of non-stop sexual pleasure hadn't even put a dent in her nymphomania.

She toed her sandals off, stretched her feet out in the grass and watched him. She knew he wasn't asleep, probably just thinking. About what? she wondered. Funny, they'd spent two whole weeks together and yet what did she really know about him? Apart from the fact that he wasn't looking for a long-term girlfriend, he had more charm and charisma than was feasible and he owned a very successful property development company. But as soon as she'd asked herself the question, a series of pictures flooded her mind like a living photo album. The way he'd tucked into his hot dog at Coney Island and

icked the mustard off his thumb with the same amount of
relish as he gave to the meal he'd devoured at a five-star restaurant. The way he'd dropped change into the tin of every
pan-handler and vagrant they passed. How relaxed he looked
in both a designer suit and his favourite faded jeans. The
sound of his terrible off-key whistle in the shower. Or how he
never failed to compliment her on whatever she was wearing,
usually before he stripped it off her. So what did that say about
him? Generous to a fault, compassionate with those less for-
tunate than himself, definitely not a snob, great taste, completely insatiable and tone deaf.

But so much more about him was still a mystery. Their conversations had always been deliberately light and teasing and
superficial. He didn't talk about his past and she didn't talk
about hers. She'd thought that was the way it had to be, for
both their sakes.

But now, with less than twenty-four hours left together, she
wasn't so sure. Because she had to admit she was desperately
curious to know more about him. Ever since she'd tended him
through those hideous night terrors the first night they'd been
together, she'd wondered about him, what had formed him.

She sighed. *Forget it, Daisy. You know what they say
about curiosity and the cat. You'd be better off leaving well
enough alone.*

She heard a shout and looked up to see a father throwing a
ball to his two sons a few feet away. She concentrated on their
game to stop her mind straying into more dangerous territory.

She smiled, noticing the way the older boy kept trying to
push his younger brother out of the way, and how the father
gently intervened. The sight made her heart squeeze. She
wondered what kind of father Connor might have made if his
last girlfriend had been pregnant after all. She chuckled. He'd
probably have a heart attack if she asked him.

'What's so funny?'

She looked down to see Connor watching her, propped up

on his elbow, his sunglasses thrown off on the grass and a curious smile on his face. She flushed and tried to think of an innocuous answer.

She nodded across the field to the man and his sons. 'I was just thinking what a wonderful dad he is.'

Connor craned his neck, leaning back on his elbows to watch. Then made a scoffing sound. 'How do you know he's a good father?'

It seemed self-evident to her, but she decided to humour him. 'Because he's being so fair with his two sons. And he really enjoys their company. When I have children, I'll want them to have a father like that. Someone as involved and committed as I am.' The words slipped out on a wistful sigh.

Connor's eyebrows lifted. '*When* you have children?'

'Well, yes.' She blushed, thinking she might have said too much, then thought, *What the heck?* This had been her dream for a long time, why should she keep it a secret? 'I've always wanted a family, a big happy family. In my opinion it's what makes life worth living.'

He watched her for what felt like an eternity, not saying a word. 'Is that what your own was like, then? Your family? Your father?'

The personal question stunned her a little. They'd both been avoiding them so carefully up till now. 'I never knew him.' She shrugged. 'But I was hardly deprived—there was never any shortage of pretend dads.'

His eyes narrowed. 'Pretend dads?'

She gave a laugh, trying for casual but getting brittle instead. 'My mother was the original born-again Bohemian—addicted to the idea of being in love. So she'd fall madly in love with some guy, we'd move in with him and then she'd discover he didn't love her—or not enough. I had a lot of what I called pretend dads as a result.' Why had she brought this up? Thinking about all those men who hadn't wanted to be her father, to be anyone's father, had always made her feel a little inadequate, and very insecure. 'None of them were horrible or anything like that. They all tried to be nice. But they weren't my father—and they didn't want to be.'

'That must have been tough,' he said gently.

His astuteness surprised her and made her feel unpleasantly vulnerable. 'I suppose it was at first,' she said, not sure she could cope with the sympathy in his eyes. 'When I was really little, I used to make the mistake of getting attached to them and then I'd be devastated when they left. But after a while I realised none of my mother's relationships would ever last. After that I forced myself not to get too attached and it was easier.'

Connor sat up, a strange tightness in his chest. She'd just given him an insight into her life he shouldn't really want. He'd been working overtime in the last week to make sure neither of them had too much time to think. He'd nearly blown things wide open at the gallery. And he still didn't know what had possessed him to introduce Daisy as his fiancée to Jessie and Monroe.

So he'd decided that night, when she'd looked so wounded, so unhappy, that the best thing to do was to keep things upbeat and not make any stupid mistakes again. Not to talk about feelings and emotions and any of that serious stuff that might complicate things.

But somehow, watching her now, hearing the hurt when she talked about all those pretend dads who'd rejected her, he felt the urge to comfort her, to make it right.

He gave his head a rueful shake as he studied her. 'Damn, Daisy, who'd have thought it?' He brushed his thumb down her cheek, felt her shiver. 'Who'd have thought my practical, steadfast little Daisy would be such a dreamer?' He forced a smile onto his lips, desperate to keep the situation light.

She took hold of his hand, pulled it down from her face. 'Why are you smiling?' she asked, and he could see the shadow of hurt in her eyes. 'What's so funny about the fact that I want a family? Just because you don't, it hardly gives you the right to laugh at me.'

'I'm not laughing. I don't think it's funny. What it is, is sweet and incredibly naive.'

'Why naive?' she said warily.

'Because you're looking for something you'll never find. There's no such thing as happy ever after. Your mother didn't find it because it was never there.' He sighed, then nodded at the spot across the meadow where the father was still playing with his sons, the old bitterness assailing him. 'How do you know yer man over there doesn't get drunk every once in a while and take his belt to those boys?'

She drew in a sharp breath. 'Why would you think that?' she whispered, her eyes wide with shock.

He shrugged but the movement felt stiff. 'Because it happens.'

'Your father did that to you, didn't he?' she said softly.

His heart slammed into his ribcage. 'How would you know that?' he said, carefully.

Seeing the compassion, the concern in her face, he wondered why the hell he'd started this conversation.

'You talk in your sleep, Connor, when you're having the nightmares.' Daisy watched his jaw tighten, the cocky smile gone from his face. And her heart bled for him. 'And I've seen the scars on your back.' But how many more scars, she wondered, did he have on his heart?

Jessie had said his attitude to family, to kids, was all mixed up in his past. She knew she shouldn't pry, that she really had no right to pry, but suddenly she just wanted to know. She'd accepted that this had to be a temporary fling, because he wasn't looking for permanent, and she couldn't change that. But suddenly she wanted to know why. Why would he want to deny himself the one thing in life that really mattered?

'Will you tell me about it?'

He gave a half-laugh, but it had a hollow ring that stabbed at Daisy's chest. 'There's nothing much to tell,' he said. 'My mother died. Left my Da on his own with six kids.' His Adam's apple bobbed as he swallowed. 'He came home that night from the hospital, cried like a baby and got blind drunk. And after that everything changed.' He plucked some grass up, rubbed it between his fingers.

She waited, a part of her scared to hear what he had to say, a part of her desperate to know so she could understand. 'How did it change?' she said gently.

He dropped the grass, rubbed his hands on his jeans. 'First off it was no more than a back hand to the head, or a punch now and again you weren't expecting. But then it was the flat of his belt, the heel of his boot, until you passed out. The drink changed him and he couldn't control it.'

Tears spilled over Daisy's lids, but she wiped them hastily away; from the monotone of his voice she could tell he didn't want her sympathy.

'My brother Mac and me, we'd wait at the window, watch for him. Mac would make the tea, and I'd bathe the girls, get them fed and tucked in before he got home. On a good night, he'd be so locked he could barely walk, so we'd feed him and pour him into bed and that would be the end of it. But on a bad night…' He paused. His eyes met hers. 'That's not happy families, Daisy. That's barely living.'

She cradled his cheek in her palm, desperate to give what little comfort she could. 'I'm so sorry, Connor.'

He pulled away, instantly defensive. 'There's nothing to be sorry for.'

'No child should have to endure that. Not ever.'

He caught a tear on his thumb, wiped it away. 'Don't, Daisy. It's not a bad story, not really. I got out. I made a life for myself apart from all that. A life I'm happy with.'

But it's only half a life, she wanted to say. Couldn't he see that? 'What happened to Mac and your sisters?'

'My…' He stopped, and for the first time since he'd started talking she saw the raw flash of remembered pain. But he collected himself quickly and it was gone. 'The authorities found out what had been going on. We got separated… Fostered and adopted.'

'Did you manage to keep in touch?'

'No. I've not seen them since. But Mac's a movie actor now. Goes by his full name of Cormac.'

'Cormac Brody?' Daisy blinked. She couldn't believe it. 'Your brother's Cormac Brody?' His brother was the Irish actor who'd taken Hollywood by storm in the last few years? Now she thought about it, she could see the resemblance. Both Connor and his brother had the same piercing blue eyes and dark good looks—and that devil-may-care charm. 'But if you know that why haven't you contacted him? Surely his agent would—'

'Why would I?' he interrupted her. 'He's not part of my life and I'm not part of his. I missed him for a while.' He shrugged, his apparent indifference stunning her. 'Just like I missed all of them, but they were better off without me and I was better off without them.'

'But that's not true,' she said, unable to bear the brittle cynicism in his voice. 'Everyone should have a family. You need them. They're part of you.'

'Daisy, don't,' he said, lifting her chin between his thumb and forefinger. 'It is true. It's the way I want it. Sure, when I was little I used to lie awake nights, praying to Our Lady that my mammy would come back. That my Da would stop drinking. That everything would go back to how it was and we could all be a happy family again. But I learned a valuable lesson. You can't go back, you can only go forward. And you can't rely on anyone. Nothing's certain. Nothing lasts. Life gets in the way, good and bad. Like you got in my way. So we enjoy it while it lasts and take everything we can grab. And that's enough.'

But it wasn't enough, she thought. Not nearly enough. Not for anyone.

He put his arm around her shoulders as they walked back across the park. As the sun dipped towards dusk, giving the fairy castle a golden glow, Daisy considered all the things he'd told her and felt her fantasy collapse and reality come flooding in.

So now she knew. Connor lived in the moment, shunned responsibility and had persuaded himself that family wasn't for him, not because he was selfish, or shallow, or self-absorbed, but because of that abused traumatised little boy who had been forced to grow up too soon, and shoulder a responsibility that should never have been his.

He wasn't scared of commitment, she realised. He was just scared of taking a chance, scared of wanting something that could blow up in his face all over again.

What a couple of cowards they both were.

Because while he'd been scared to take a chance, she'd been so scared of making her mother's mistakes she'd side-stepped, and avoided and denied the obvious all along.

That she was falling hopelessly in love with him.

She bit into her lip, determined not to let her emotional turmoil show as the enormity of what she'd just admitted to herself sank in.

Oh, God, what on earth was she going to do now?

CHAPTER FOURTEEN

As CONNOR stood beside her in a perfectly tailored tuxedo like her own Prince Charming, Daisy let her eyes wander over the magnificent ballroom and began to wonder how much more surreal her life could become. Chandeliers cast a shimmering light on the assembled throng. Women preened like peacocks in their latest designer plumage and men looked important and debonair in their dark dinner suits. The ball was an annual event hosted by the New York Governor for some deserving charity, but according to Connor it was really just an excuse for the state's most prominent citizens to show off.

The necklace he'd given her felt cool against her cleavage, matching the emerald satin gown she'd hastily put together on her second-hand sewing machine a lifetime ago. Daisy took a deep breath, and rested her hand on Connor's sleeve, trying to get her balance. Ever since they'd got back from the park her emotions had been in uproar, her senses reeling. But she had managed to make one important decision this evening. She planned to live the last of her grand adventure tonight to the max. She'd have time enough tomorrow to panic about her wayward heart.

'Daisy, that dress is sensational.'

Daisy turned to see Jessie Latimer, a champagne flute in her hand and a friendly grin on her face. 'Where ever did you get it?' she said. 'Enquiring minds want to know.'

'I…' She hesitated, wondering if it was the done thing to admit you'd made your own ball gown.

'She made it herself.' Connor smoothed his hand over the ruched satin at her hip and hugged her to his side, his gaze darkening with appreciation. 'Not just gorgeous but talented too,' he murmured against her neck.

Daisy could feel the pulse hammering in her throat as Jessie gave her a pointed look over Connor's shoulder.

'That's amazing,' she said. 'Listen, Daisy, I've told my sister Ali all about you and I'd love you to meet her. Actually, it's sort of a mercy mission.' She took Daisy's hand. 'She found out yesterday she's expecting again and she's in a state of shock. I need you to help take her mind off it.'

Daisy acknowledged the little prickle of envy and ignored it. She'd have her big happy family one day. She'd make sure of it. 'I'd love to meet her,' she said, and meant it. A little time spent away from Connor wouldn't necessarily be a bad thing. It might help her get her heart rate under control in preparation for the night ahead.

Connor gave a mock shudder. 'Ali's pregnant again? What's that? Number four?'

Jessie nodded, giving Daisy's hand a tug. 'Actually the doctor said it may be number four and five. She's so huge already. Hence the shock.'

Connor frowned as Daisy stepped out of his arms. 'Wait a minute. Why don't I come over? I can congratulate her.'

Jessie pushed her finger into his chest. 'This is strictly girls only, big boy. Linc and Monroe are over by the bar trying to finesse a couple of beers out of the barman. Go play with them.'

As Jessie led her through the crowd of Manhattan's elite Daisy couldn't resist a glance over her shoulder at Connor. Her heartbeat slowed and her stomach tightened. He still stood where she'd left him, looking impossibly dashing in the middle of the crowded ballroom in his black tuxedo with an irritated frown on his face and his hands thrust into his pockets as he watched her go.

She heaved out a breath. Okay, she was falling in love, but that didn't mean she had to get stupid. All she had to do now was keep the brakes on, enjoy tonight and then confront him tomorrow. See where she stood. Maybe she'd fallen for her romantic fairy tale, but it didn't mean she couldn't still be practical, sensible. Love might be blind, but it didn't have to turn you into an idiot. She still knew what she wanted out of life and, whatever Connor's reasons, he'd made it very clear that afternoon he didn't want the same things. Unless he was falling in love with her too, that wasn't going to change.

'There's definitely something to be said for a bad boy in a tux,' Jessie said quietly, interrupting Daisy's latest strategy briefing.

Daisy's head whipped round. The considering look in Jessie's eyes spoke volumes: Daisy had been staring at Connor for far too long. 'Yes, I suppose so,' she said, trying for practical and getting breathless instead.

'How's it going? We don't have to meet Ali. I just thought you might like a little downtime before the dancing begins. You both look a little shell-shocked. Did something happen?'

She was certainly shell-shocked, she thought. But she wasn't so sure about Connor. She'd caught him watching her, a wary, cautious look in his eyes when they'd been in the cab coming back from the park. That look was the reason she'd decided not to blurt out how she felt. Why ruin the mood before she was absolutely sure? And anyway, she'd wanted to have tonight to add to her memories before it all went belly up, as she was fast suspecting it would. He might need a family, but he didn't necessarily need her. What on earth did she really have to offer him that he couldn't get from a hundred other, much more sophisticated women?

'Don't be silly,' Daisy said, almost choking on the fake bonhomie. 'Nothing's wrong.' Well, not yet. 'This is all just a bit much for a girl from Portobello Road, that's all.'

'Yes, the Americans do excess so well, don't you think?' Jessie smiled back, but Daisy could see she was being kind and letting her off the hook. 'Oh, good grief!' Jessie said, her eyes lighting on something over Daisy's shoulder. 'That woman is a complete menace. Poor Lincoln had to peel her off him ten minutes ago and now she's got Connor in her sights.'

Daisy looked round. All the colour drained out of her face and then pumped back into her cheeks. Wrapped around Connor like a second skin was a pneumatic blonde with a skirt that barely covered her butt and boobs that could poke someone's eye out.

He still had his hands in his pockets, and his body language didn't suggest he was enjoying the encounter all that much, but as the woman leaned closer to whisper something in his ear he took one hand out and rested it on her waist.

A red haze blurred Daisy's vision. 'Who is she?' she asked, her voice calm despite the volcanic eruption bubbling beneath her breastbone.

Doesn't she know he's engaged? she almost added. Then realised her mistake. The molten magma got hotter.

'Mitzi Melrose, the biggest flirt on the planet,' Jessie said. 'Her husband's Eldridge Melrose, billionaire financier, and I don't think he's got what it takes to satisfy our Mitzi if her relentless poaching is anything…' Jessie's voice slowly receded until all Daisy could hear was the buzzing of a thousand chainsaws, her gaze transfixed on her fake fiancé and the floozy.

The Botoxed bimbo was leaning into him now, her pillar-box lips practically touching his ear lobe and her gravity-defying cleavage as good as propped on his forearm.

And, as far as Daisy could tell, Connor wasn't doing a damn thing about it. He'd taken his hand off her hip, sure, stuck it back in his pocket, but he hadn't moved away, had he? She'd never been the jealous type, even with Gary, who'd been an inveterate flirt. Daisy, being the practical, sensible, focussed woman she was, had always thought that possessive women who couldn't trust their partners were creatures to be pitied. But right at this moment she could sympathise with them completely.

She had Connor's ring on her finger. Maybe it was a temporary ring and a fake engagement, but, still, she'd worn it because he'd asked her, she'd let him introduce her to everyone as his bride-to-be and now he had another woman glued to his torso. And if that weren't bad enough, he'd made her fall in love with him, the stupid dolt.

'Jessie, you'll have to excuse me for a minute,' she said, still glaring at her non-fiancé.

'Go for it,' she heard Jessie say with a suspicious lift in her voice. But Daisy didn't have time to process it as she sailed back through the crowd propelled on a wave of righteous anger, the surge of adrenaline making her heartbeat pound in her ears and her skin flush red.

She'd been an idiot. She'd lived in the moment, soaked up every single speck of excitement and in the process lost a crucial part of herself. She was her own woman. And yet, somehow or other, she'd ended up letting Connor call all the shots. He'd got her to New York, he'd got her back in his bed, he'd put his ring on her finger and what had she got? Quite possibly a broken heart, that was what. Fine, she'd deal with that if she had to, but he was not going to get away with pawing another woman in public when he was supposed to be engaged to her. The engagement might be fake, but her feelings were real. She might not have his love, but she intended to have his respect.

His head lifted as she walked towards him, as if he'd sensed her approach, those magnetic eyes fixed on her face and he smiled.

He might as well have pulled out a red bandanna and waved it in front of her nose. What, she'd like to know, was so flipping amusing?

Connor tuned out Mitzi's breathy whisper. His heart pounded as he watched the satin gown Daisy had made shimmer, spotlighting those provocative curves to perfection. He couldn't make out her expression in the muted lighting, but the vision of high cheekbones, fine, alabaster skin and glossy red curls made all his senses stand up and pay attention. His annoyance and impatience dimmed, to be replaced by a rush of longing that he didn't understand—and didn't want to understand.

Even though she was still several feet away he could have sworn he could smell that spicy, erotic scent of hers, and feel the soft swell of her breasts beneath his fingertips.

The truth was, he'd never been a fan of networking, of getting all spruced up and showing himself off. But ever since Daisy had walked out of their bedroom earlier decked out in the ball gown, the green satin hugging her curves and making him ache in some very interesting places, the thought of going to the Governor's Ball and mingling with people he didn't give a hoot about had become considerably less appealing.

What he'd wanted to do was stay in their suite and make love to her for the rest of the evening, then listen to her talk—he adored how she drifted from topic to topic without pausing for breath in that practical, no-nonsense way she had—and then he'd planned to fall asleep with her head pillowed on his chest.

But after all the things he'd told her in the park, he'd been forced to dismiss the idea. He'd let things get too serious again without intending to, telling her things he shouldn't about his past, and then, to top it all, he'd seen the tenderness, the longing in her eyes when he'd put his arm on her shoulders and he wasn't sure what to make of it. She hadn't challenged him about what he'd said, she'd simply accepted it—but he'd been waiting for the axe to fall ever since. For her to tell him how wrong he was for her. For her to throw his past back in his face. For her to demand more from him than he could ever give. But she hadn't done it, and it was making him crazy.

But once they'd been in the limo, her seductive scent tantalising him, he'd finally had to face the fact that he wasn't going to be able to let her go when they returned to England tomorrow as he'd planned. He'd thought that if he sated himself on her during these two weeks in New York, he'd be well over his infatuation by now, but she still captivated him as much, if not more, than she had the first time they'd made love.

She was less than five paces away from him when the chandelier illuminated her face at last. He could see anger and determination swirling in those expressive emerald eyes, and his stomach pitched. Had the penny finally dropped? Was she about to give him the boot?

He clamped down on the sudden surge of panic, the strangling feeling of pain and regret closing his throat. That was too bad. Because whatever was going on between them, it wasn't over. He still had unfinished business with her and if she thought he was going to let her dump him, she'd have to think again.

'Hi, Connor, why don't you introduce me to your new best friend?' Daisy said sweetly. Sweetly enough to cause tooth decay.

The bimbo had her hand on his lapel now. Daisy's fingers clenched into a fist. She resisted the urge to slug the woman. But only just.

Connor looked momentarily confused, then glanced at the bimbo. 'Oh, yeah, Mitzi, this is Daisy Dean, my fiancée. Do you think you could leave us be for—?'

Mitzi cut off whatever he was going to say with an ear-splitting giggle. 'Your fiancée? You've got to be kidding me.' Her high-pitched voice piped out like Marilyn Monroe on helium. 'You never said you were getting married, sweetie.' She pressed one of her scarlet-tipped talons against Connor's cheek and giggled again before sending Daisy a smile filled with enough malice to make Mussolini look like a pussycat. 'Why, I guess it must have slipped his mind, we were having such a good time and all.' She shoved her expertly moulded breasts forward. 'But then men get distracted so easily, don't they, honey?'

Screw restraint. Daisy wasn't taking *that* lying down. 'Yes, they do.' She smiled sharply. 'Especially when they're being smothered in enough cheap perfume to fell an ox.'

Mitzi's jaw dropped comically. 'Huh?'

'Daisy, what's got into you?' Connor said, gripping her arm and stepping to her side.

She thrust her chin up, willing her bottom lip to stop quivering. 'Oh, I don't know, Connor. Maybe it's that you're wrapped around her when you're supposed to be engaged to me.'

He looked at her as if she were talking in tongues. 'Whoah?'

And she lost it. So this was what it boiled down to, she thought, as her fury—with herself as well as him—raged out of control.

He whisked her off to New York, he told everyone they were a couple, he said things to her she was sure he'd never said to anyone else and he made love to her with a power and a passion that made her lose her grip on reality. But when push came to shove, it had all been a game—at least for him. She was just another of the women he'd charmed into bed.

'You heard me, Connor. Either you respect me. Or you don't. You can't have it both ways.'

'I paid a grand a bottle for this stuff, you little bitch,' Mitzi shrieked.

'Shut up, Mitzi!' he snarled.

'I'm gonna tell my husband about this,' Mitzi squeaked as she shrank back. 'Don't you think I won't and you can kiss that damn deal goodbye.'

'Be my guest, now get lost.' He threw the words over his shoulder, his eyes still fixed on Daisy's face.

The woman flounced off with an audible huff and Daisy became aware of the silence around them. At least twenty pairs of eyes were fixed on their little theatrical display.

'Now why don't you tell me what the hell is going on here?' Connor announced, as if she were a naughty child, completely oblivious to their audience.

Daisy tried to step away from him, humiliation swamping her. But he was still holding her arm.

Oh, God, what had she done? She'd let her anger and uncertainty take over and now she'd made a complete spectacle of herself. But as if that weren't bad enough, Connor was looking at her as if she'd lost her marbles. She felt the tears sting her eyes and pushed them back. It was so grossly unfair. Why did she have to be the one to fall in love?

She bit the sob back. Forget it, she wasn't going to cry over him. And definitely not with all these people watching. 'Let go of my arm. I want to go back to the hotel,' she whispered. 'We're making a scene.'

'The hell with that.' He took her other arm, pulled her close despite her struggles. 'You're going to tell me what you meant. Of course I respect you—how could I not?'

'I'm not talking about this. Not now.' Not ever. It would just humiliate her more. He wasn't going to make her break.

'Oh, yes, you are. I'm sick of waiting for you to say it.'

Waiting for her to say what? But before she could figure out what the heck he was talking about, he clamped his hand on her wrist and started dragging her through the crowd. A sea of heads turned to stare at them both as he marched her out of the ballroom. She'd never been more mortified in her life. But what was worse, much worse, was the thought that he might make her crack and reveal everything—and then she'd be completely at his mercy.

He slammed into the ladies' powder room. The elderly matron busy fluffing her hair in front of the ornate mirror glanced up.

'Why, Connor Brody,' she said. Daisy blinked. Had the old dame just batted her eyelids at him? 'What are you doing in the Ladies' Lounge, you bad boy?'

Connor smiled back, giving her the full blast of his lethal Celtic charm. Daisy barely resisted the urge to kick him. First Mitzi and now a woman three times his age. Did he never know when to turn it off?

'Mrs Gildenstern, it's a pleasure.'

Good God, she'd fallen for the playboy of the Western World. Daisy snorted indignantly, but they both ignored her.

'I need a moment with my fiancée in private,' he said.

'So this is the lucky girl?' the woman purred, fluffing her hair some more and sending Daisy a flirtatious wink. She got up and touched Connor's arm. 'You go right ahead, my boy,' she said. 'I'll make sure no one disturbs you.' Her paper-thin skin crinkled as she grinned. 'But don't you two get up to anything I wouldn't,' she finished as she left the room, chortling like a naughty schoolgirl.

'Sure, thanks, Mrs G,' Connor finished distractedly. He turned to Daisy, all traces of that industrial-strength charm wiped out by a dark scowl. 'Now I want to know what's going on.'

'I don't need to tell you a thing.'

'Oh, yeah.' He pressed her back against the vanity unit, hard thighs trapping her hips, hot hands clamping on the exposed skin of her back and the smell of soap and pheromones overwhelming her. 'Think again. Because you're not getting out of here till you do.'

The warm spot between her legs pulsed hot. She slapped her hands against his chest, and shoved. He barely budged. She glared at him some more. He didn't even flinch.

'I didn't like seeing you paw that floozy,' she said grudgingly. 'But now I'm over it.' *Almost.*

'What floozy? You mean Mitzi?' he said, sounding so astonished the old red rag popped out again and ruined all her best intentions.

'Yes Mitzi. I mean, I know this relationship is a sham. I know we're only pretending to be engaged.' When exactly had she lost sight of that? 'But if you could refrain from smooching with other women in public I'd appreciate it. I happen to have some pride, you know.' Although she'd lost sight of that too somewhere. 'Just because I don't have mile-long legs and breasts that will still be perky when I'm dead. As far as

everyone here is concerned I *am* your fiancée and that ought
to entitle me to a tiny iota of your respect.'

Now she sounded pathetic too. She wanted to kill him.
How had he managed to turn her into a desperate, grasping,
needy nutcase that she didn't even recognise?

His scowl deepened momentarily and then his eyebrows
kicked up. 'Jesus. You're jealous,' he murmured incredulously.

'I am not jealous,' she shot back. 'That would make me an
imbecile.' Wouldn't it just?

'Yes, you are,' he said, flashing her that megawatt grin. The
satisfied gleam in his eyes lit Daisy's temper up like a Chinese
firecracker.

'That does it. I'm out of here.' She struggled, but he simply
grabbed her waist and held her still. Then his thumbs slipped
under the satin of her gown, trailing goosebumps in their
wake. She gasped.

'I've got to tell you,' he murmured, his fingers caressing
bare skin as his hands wrapped round her, 'you're magnificent when you're mad, angel.' He chuckled, the sound throaty
and self-satisfied and wholely male.

Fury engulfed her. She was not going to get sidetracked,
not again.

'Don't you dare laugh at me,' she said, 'or I'll slug you.'

She freed her arm and tried to take aim, but he caught her
fist in his, laughing as he kissed her knuckles. 'Now, now,
angel. Don't get nasty.'

Then she felt it, the solid length of his arousal, outlined against
the soft swell of her belly. Heat spiralled from her core and she
struggled in earnest. 'No. No way,' she yelped, staring into his
eyes and seeing the intent on his face. 'Forget it. We are not
making love. If you haven't noticed, we're having an argument.'

'Pay attention, angel,' he said as his clever fingers whisked
down the zip on her dress. 'We've had the argument.' The
bodice fell away, baring her lacy push-up bra. 'And we're
about to have the make-up sex.'

'But we're in the powder room. We can't,' she shouted, frantic and afraid and already so turned on she was sure she was about to explode.

This wasn't possible. It couldn't be happening. She'd never made love in a public place before. 'We can't, anyone could walk in,' she said, her voice rising in panic as he pushed her bra up.

'Don't worry, no one messes with Mrs G,' he said, weighing her breast in his palm.

'But what if Mrs Gildenstern dies of a heart attack?' she blurted out, her voice rising in panic as his fingers played havoc. 'What if the fire alarm goes off? What if the SAS storms the building?'

He fastened hot lips on her nipple, suckled strongly. She choked out a sob as he teased and bit the engorged peak—and every single coherent thought flew right out of her head.

She threaded her fingers through his hair, held on as her head bumped the mirror and she gave herself up to the fireball of sensations.

He lifted her panting onto the vanity unit, brushed his hands up her legs under the billowing satin and plunged his fingers into the heart of her.

'I want you, Daisy. More than I've ever wanted any woman.' He stroked the slick folds of her sex as she bucked against his hand. Then his lips took hers in a kiss so passionate, she could taste his vicious arousal matching her own.

She stared dumbly, her body trembling with need as he pulled the condom out of his breast pocket with unsteady fingers and freed himself from his trousers.

She whimpered as he held her hips, pushed her panties to one side and entered her in one long, relentless thrust. As she clung to him all her thoughts, all her feelings, centred on the exquisite joy pulsating through her. She rode on the crest for an eternity as his powerful strokes took him deeper. She heard his low groan, felt his shoulders stiffen as she took that last wild leap into oblivion.

Her fingers trembled on the damp curls at his nape, her senses spinning as she listened to the ragged pants of their breathing and her thundering heartbeat, the sounds harsh and uncivilised against the soft strains of music from the ballroom beyond.

He lifted his head and his eyes met hers—determination making the deep blue of his irises glow with purpose.

'This isn't over. Not yet.' His hands stroked her thighs, squeezed. 'You know that, right?'

She could hear the urgency in his voice, the yearning, and her heart swelled with hope. 'I know,' she whispered.

She felt herself plunging into the chasm—but knew she wasn't falling in love any more, she'd fallen.

CHAPTER FIFTEEN

DAISY slept fitfully on the flight home, despite the flat bed, the world-class service and the fact that she was physically and mentally exhausted from the emotional roller-coaster ride her life had somehow become. She couldn't even get a good firm grip on all the 'what ifs' whirring about in her mind, let alone answer any of them.

What if she told him she loved him and he looked angry? What if she told him and he looked bored? What if he thought she was delusional? What if she was?

She resigned herself to the fact that whatever happened she would have to tell him, because the 'what ifs' would drive her completely doolally if she didn't. And then she started stressing over the 'When'. Eventually she fell asleep over Nova Scotia, Connor's hand resting on her hip, knowing that when she got home she would have to face one of the toughest conversations of her life. But she promised herself, whatever happened, she would not wimp out—and she wouldn't let Connor wimp out either. He was going to have to come up with something a bit more substantial than, 'Not Yet'.

'Wake up, angel. We're home.'

The minute he'd said the H word, Connor felt the little spurt of panic.

Don't be an idiot, it's an expression. It doesn't mean a thing.

He shook Daisy again, leaned down to kiss her cheek. Her lids fluttered open, her eyes fixing on his face. He felt the twist in his chest as he stared into the mermaid green, and the spurt got worse.

Why couldn't he let her go?

He'd been awake during the whole of their transatlantic flight, her lush body curled up next to his, trying to figure it out. She hadn't gone the route of most females and tried to pin him down. That had to be it. As soon as she did the honeymoon period would be over. But a moment ago, when the car had pulled up at the house in Portobello, and he'd turned to see Daisy by his side, he'd begun to wonder if he wasn't in serious trouble. She'd snuck under his guard somehow—and he didn't like it.

'Mmm…' She stretched, giving him a peek of the purple lace of her bra through the buttonholes of her blouse. He felt the familiar punch of lust.

And why did he still want her? All the damn time? Had she put some kind of spell on him?

'Are we home?' she asked around a jaw-breaking yawn.

And there was that H word again. He didn't like it.

'Yeah.' He pushed back, stepped out of the limo. Maybe he needed to get away from her for a while, take a time-out. But even as he thought of letting her go, even for just one night, her hand clasped his as she stepped out of the car and he knew he couldn't do it. The spurt became a flood.

The chauffeur deposited their luggage on the kerb, tipped his hat. 'Would you like me to take them into the house, sir?'

'No, that's grand,' he said, dragging a roll of bills from his pocket and flicking out a tenner. 'Thanks for your help, Joe.'

He watched the long black Mercedes drive away and settled on his course of action. He'd keep her with him for the next little while. He wanted her with him, in his house. But he'd make damn sure she didn't get any closer. She was too close already.

He shoved one of the smaller suitcases under his arm, picked up the two larger. 'Let's take these up to mine. We need to talk.'

She blinked lids still heavy with sleep, her cheeks coloured. 'You know?' she said.

'Know what?' he asked.

Then she looked past him, her eyes widening, and all the pink leached out of her face. The small carry-on bag she carried clattered onto the pavement.

'What's that?' she asked, pointing past him.

He glanced over his shoulder and spotted the For Sale sign. He'd forgotten all about his conversation with the estate agent three weeks ago. He turned back and saw the horror on her face and the sparkle of unshed tears. Something fierce and protective clasped his heart—and not for the first time.

'You're moving out?' she said, her voice so quiet he could barely hear it.

His first instinct was to tell her he wasn't. He didn't want to any more. But the minute the need to calm and to nurture welled up inside him, the panic closed around his throat. What was wrong with him? He didn't want anything permanent. He didn't need the responsibility. He'd had permanent before, he'd had responsibility and he'd failed at it spectacularly. He couldn't risk it again. This was his get-out clause. He couldn't afford to throw it away.

He shrugged, forced himself to ignore the misery in her eyes. 'Sure. But with the market as it is, it'll take a while to sell.' Long enough, he hoped, for him to get over this infatuation once and for all. 'Until then we can continue to enjoy each other. It's been fun so far,' he said, struggling to keep the seductive smile in place.

Daisy felt as if she'd been punched in the gut.

He was selling the house, moving out, and he hadn't even bothered to tell her? And he was looking at her now, his face calm and nonchalant, as if to say, 'Why would I?' It was the same stubborn look he'd had on his face when she'd asked him why he had never contacted his movie-star brother. She looked down at the ring he'd given her and realised just how delusional she'd allowed herself to get.

She gulped down the tears tightening her throat, straightened her spine. 'No, thanks. I'd rather make a clean break,' she said. 'Here.' She tugged the silver band loose and held it out to him. 'I should give this back to you.'

His jaw tightened as he looked down at the ring. He put the suitcases down, but made no move to take it. 'Come on, angel. Don't overreact. This isn't a big deal.'

Maybe not to him, she thought, her heart shattering inside her. Her fingers curled around the ring and she felt the tiny diamonds cut into her palm.

'Actually it is a big deal. Because I've fallen in love with you, you stupid moron.' It wasn't exactly how she'd planned to tell him, but even so his reaction was worse than any she could have imagined.

His mouth dropped open and his skin paled beneath the tan. 'Whoah, what's that now?'

Horrified. He looked horrified. Well, at least she had the answer to her 'What if'.

Biting down on her lips so hard she tasted blood, she lifted his hand and slapped the ring into it. 'It's okay, Connor. It's my mistake. I'll go quietly. I'm not even going to make a scene.'

She thought of all the scenes her mother had made, all the scenes she'd had to witness over the years, and forced the vicious pain back, buried it deep. The only thing she had left was pride—and she couldn't afford to throw it away, because she had a feeling she was going to need it.

She picked up her bag to leave, but he took her arm, pulled her round to face him.

'What's this now? You don't love me. That's rubbish. Since when?'

He didn't sound horrified any more; he sounded angry. He wasn't the only one.

'Don't tell me how I feel. I do love you, Connor. But you know what? I'm not asking for anything in return. Especially as it's pretty obvious you don't want to give it to me.'

She yanked her arm out of his, but he grabbed her back. 'Hold on a minute. You can't tell me you love me then storm off. That's madness.'

'Yes, I can, because you don't love me back,' she shouted, then realised she was making a scene after all. Damn it. 'Well, do you?' she whispered.

He flinched and she felt nausea churn in her stomach.

'I don't love anyone,' he said. 'I'm no good at it.' Was that supposed to make her feel better? 'I don't want this. I told you that.'

She shook her head, the tears choking her. 'I know you did, Connor.' And he had, he had told her. And it was her own stupid fault that she hadn't listened. Or rather, she'd listened with her heart, instead of her head, and she'd got it wrong.

Daisy sighed, suddenly desperately weary, and sick to her heart as well as her stomach.

'Don't worry, Connor. I'll survive. I'll see you around.'

She turned but he called after her. 'Daisy, don't go. Let's at least talk about this some more.'

Didn't he know there was nothing else to say?

She waved over her shoulder. 'I'll be around, maybe later,' she said. Knowing full well that she'd be conveniently absent if he came to call. She'd do whatever she had to do to avoid him over the coming weeks—until he lost interest and moved on to his next conquest—and in the meantime she'd try to repair her heart.

As she walked the few short steps to her home, the sound of her suitcase wheels rolling on the pavement matching the click-click of her heels, she felt her stomach pitch—and refused to look back. She had never felt more bitterly ashamed of herself in her life.

Despite all her care over the years, despite all her caution.

She'd got caught in the same foolish trap as her mother—of falling in love with the wrong guy, and hoping against all the odds that he might love her back. And he hadn't.

Connor dropped the suitcases on the floor and slammed the door shut. Well, that hadn't exactly gone according to plan. And where the hell had she got the stupid idea she loved him? It was insane.

He dumped his keys on the hall table, saw the stack of post, left it where it lay and walked down the hallway.

She'd get over it soon enough. Things had got too hot and heavy over the last fortnight. They'd been living in each other's pockets, after all. A little while cooling off would be all for the best. And then they could pick up where they'd left off.

But as he entered the open-plan kitchen, the sunlight pouring through the windows and shining off the polished oak, his gut tightened with dread and the sense of being trapped closed over him like a shroud.

What if she wouldn't come back?

He stared at the bright airy space, the gleaming glass cabinets, and felt as if they were mocking him. He fished the ring out of his pocket, dropped it on the counter top, then gazed out into the garden where he'd first spotted her three long weeks ago.

And for the first time since he'd been a boy, he wanted to pray for something he knew he could never have.

He heaved out a sigh, pushed the ring into a drawer. This was madness. He was just jet-lagged and a little shaken by how devastated she'd looked. But she'd get over it. He'd told her the truth, after all. He didn't love her. He couldn't. He'd always sworn he would never fall in love and that would never change. But he'd get her back, because he wanted her and he knew damn well she still wanted him.

But even as he tried to persuade himself there was nothing

to worry about he had the niggling feeling that he'd let something irreplaceable slip through his fingers and there would be no getting it back, no matter how hard he tried.

CHAPTER SIXTEEN

DAISY stifled her tears as she opened her suitcase and saw all the mementoes she'd saved so carefully sitting on the top. The sweetly tacky tourist photo of her in Connor's arms atop the Empire State. The ticket stub from her first and no doubt last Broadway show. A napkin from the Rainbow Room. She also held firm as she folded away the cocktail dress and the ball gown and wondered when she'd ever get the chance to wear them again.

Having showered and changed into her work uniform of jeans and a Funky Fashionista T-shirt, she walked to the stall. Buffeted by the tide of tourists flowing through Portobello Market on a sunny Sunday morning, she ignored the ropey feeling in her stomach and the foggy feeling of exhaustion and still refused to let a single tear fall.

She'd been a fool—that was all. She could cope with this, as she'd coped with every other disappointment in her life. Her throat felt raw now, as if a boulder had got jammed down it, but this wasn't really so terrible. She'd allowed herself to get carried away. When she looked back on this, years from now, she'd see it as a valuable learning experience. Almost certainly.

She sucked in a tremulous breath, returned the wave of a stallholder she knew.

She still had her dream. One day she'd find the right man

for her. Connor had never been that man. She'd allowed the stardust and the glamour and the magic of the moment to blind her to the truth. She strolled up the busy thoroughfare, loaded with stalls selling everything from plaintains to paper-chains, crossed her arms over her chest and held in the tearing pain.

She'd get past this, and when she did she'd be able to remember her time with Connor as a dazzlingly exciting and wonderful romantic adventure and nothing more. So a tiny part of her heart would always be lost to him, would always wish that maybe things might have been different, that he might have wanted what she had to offer. But he hadn't and she'd be a fool to think she could change him. Wasn't that the mistake her mother had always made?

As she spotted her stall up ahead, the rainbow of cotton dresses and silk scarves she'd made and designed flapping in the breeze, a small smile quivered on her lips. This was her real life. And she loved it. This was what made her different from her mother. She'd sampled the drug that had driven her mother to find love in the wrong places and for two glorious weeks she'd ridden the high. But she could live without it if she had to. Steady, dependable, reliable was what she needed in her life—and she was the only one who could make that happen.

She stepped up to the stall, a brave smile firmed in place. 'Hey, got a blouse you can sell me?'

Juno's head came up. 'Daisy, you're back.' Her best friend dived round the stall, a welcoming grin on her face and her arms open wide. 'How did it go?'

But as Juno's arms folded around her, the emotions she'd been holding back so beautifully rose up like a summer storm and burst out of her mouth in a soul-drenching sob.

'Daisy, what is it? What happened? What's wrong?' She could barely hear Juno's frantic questions over the gulping cries ripping her apart.

Juno held on, patting her shoulders, whispering calming

words until the sobs subsided, the wrenching pain tightening into a ball of misery. Daisy drew back, scrubbed an impatient hand across her cheeks. 'God, I'm sorry.'

Jacie stared at her over Juno's shoulder, wide-eyed with concern. 'Blimey, Daze. What's the matter? I've never seen you cry like that. Never.'

Juno gripped her upper arms, stood back, her eyes hard. 'He did this, didn't he?'

Daisy hiccoughed, the crying jag not quite done with. 'I fell in love with him, Ju.' A final tear slipped over her lid. She brushed it away. 'What a plonker, eh?'

'Oh, Daze,' Juno said, and hauled Daisy back into her arms for another hard hug. Then she pushed her back, fixed her eyes on Daisy. 'Did you tell him how you feel?'

'Yes, I did. And he doesn't feel the same way,' Daisy said, the admission, spoken out loud, making the depression suffocate her. 'So that's the end of it.' She walked round the stall and accepted Jacie's quick hug.

'Are you sure?' Jacie questioned, ever the optimist.

'Positive,' she murmured, her voice cracking on the finality of it all.

Jacie looked ready to question her some more, but Daisy was saved by a customer eager to buy a shawl.

Juno drew her to one side. 'He's not worthy of you,' she said. 'I thought he was a total scumbag the moment I laid eyes on him. And this confirms it.'

But he wasn't a scumbag, Daisy thought. He was a good man, not the right man maybe, but still a good man. Daisy pressed her fingers to Juno's lips. 'It's okay, Juno. I'll get over him.' She sighed. 'Eventually. We just weren't right for each other. I knew that from the start and I was a fool to think anything else. Anyway.' Daisy paused, blew out a breath. 'He's selling his house, moving on, so at least I won't have to be constantly reminded of my stupidity.'

Why didn't the thought make her feel any better, though?

In fact… She slapped a hand over her mouth as the nausea rose up to gag her.

'Quick, Juno, hand me a bag,' she cried, her voice muffled. 'I'm going to be sick.'

Juno thrust one of the stall's recycled plastic shopping bags into her hand and Daisy lost the contents of her stomach.

'Daze, are you okay?' Juno rubbed her back and took the bag out of her hands. 'Here, I'll go dump this.'

Daisy groaned. She was never ill. The events of the last hour had been fairly shattering, but, honestly, wasn't it about time she started pulling herself together?

'Gosh, Daisy, how do you feel?' Jacie remarked from beside her.

Daisy put her hand to her stomach. 'Not great, actually.' How could she still feel nauseous? She'd thrown up everything she'd eaten in the last twelve hours. 'I guess it's the emotional overload.'

'Either that or you're pregnant.'

Daisy's head shot up. 'That's not even funny, Jace. Not to mention a physical impossibility.' She sighed; at least she hadn't been stupid enough to sleep with Connor without protection.

'Are you on your period, then?' Jacie's eyes dropped to her chest. 'Because your boobs look enormous.'

Daisy glanced down. Her cleavage *was* looking rather more spectacular than usual, even accounting for her push-up bra. 'It's nothing. I'm due any day now, that's all.'

Wait a minute. When was her last period? In all the excitement of the last few weeks she'd forgotten about it. But… 'What's the date?' she asked.

'The twenty-fifth,' Juno said carefully, having returned from her trip to the bin.

Daisy's blood rushed out of her head and slammed straight into her heart. She couldn't breathe. She wasn't pregnant. She couldn't be; her period was just a couple of weeks late, that was all. Even though it had never, ever been late before. She looked up into Juno's concerned face. 'I can't be pregnant. It's simply not possible. Connor always used a condom, every time.'

Juno frowned. 'You do know they're only about ninety-nine per cent reliable, right? They're not a hundred per cent.'

'I know that, but…' Daisy stopped. But what? 'We never had one break or anything like that.' She couldn't possibly have got pregnant.

'They don't necessarily have to break.' Juno sank down in the chair next to her. Her brow furrowed into ominous rows.

'Of course they do—his sperm can't get through rubber, for goodness' sake.' Daisy jerked a shoulder. 'Not unless it's supersonic or something. Can it?'

'Oh, Daze.'

Daisy swivelled round to see Jacie wearing the same worried frown as Juno.

'What? What is it?' Why were they looking at her like that?

'How late *are* you?' Juno asked gently.

'Only…' She did a quick calculation. Oh, God, she'd been due for over two weeks.

'I think we better get you a home pregnancy test,' Juno said without waiting for her answer. 'Just to be on the safe side,' she finished hopefully.

'You have to tell him, Daisy.'

Daisy's fingers fisted on the plastic stick, her whole body trembling. She had to be dreaming this, surely. Or having a nightmare. She could not be expecting Connor Brody's baby.

Juno's hand squeezed her shoulder. 'You know that, right?'

'It's not true. Maybe we should do another. There must be some mistake. He'll never believe me if I tell him. I don't believe me.'

'We've done three tests already,' her friend said. 'There's no mistake. And unless it's the immaculate conception, Mr

Superstud is the father.' Juno took a weary breath. 'You should go over there now and tell him, get it out the way. Then you can start thinking about what you're going to do.'

Daisy dropped the plastic stick on top of the others in her waste-paper bin, her mind whizzing like a Catherine wheel. The three pink plus signs floated in front of her eyes like something out of a Salvador Dali painting.

'I'm going to call Maya,' Juno whispered, her hand still gripping Daisy's shoulder. 'So you can discuss your options.'

Daisy placed her hand on her abdomen, rubbed. Her heart rate finally calmed down enough so that she could grasp one wonderful, impossible truth. 'Juno.' She looked up at her friend, tears of joy pricking her lids. 'I'm going to be a mummy.'

Tears welled in Juno's eyes too, to match the ones now flowing freely down Daisy's cheeks. 'So you're going to have it?'

Daisy nodded. 'Yes. Yes, I am. I know the circumstances are a total disaster, but I could never do anything else.'

Juno clasped her hand over Daisy's. 'Whatever happens, I'll be here to help and so will Mrs V and Jace and everyone else you know. And that's a lot of people. You're not alone.'

'I know.' Daisy nodded and sniffed. Why had she ever thought she didn't have a family?

Juno wiped the moisture away, slanted Daisy a wobbly grin. 'Enough hearts and flowers. When are you going to tell Brody?'

Daisy's heart stopped. The moment of euphoria faded to be replaced by a terrible wave of grief. 'I'm not.'

'Don't be silly. You have to tell him. He has a right to know.'

'I can't tell him,' she said dully, the awful reality of what that meant finally dawning on her.

'Are you worried he'll try and make you have an abortion?' Juno said carefully.

Daisy shook her head. 'No, he wouldn't do that.' She stared at her hands, the knuckles whitening as she twisted them in her lap. 'Actually I think he'd do the opposite.' She remembered what Jessie had told her about the pregnancy scare with his last girlfriend. 'There's a core of honesty, of goodness in him. He'll feel responsible and he'll want to do the right thing. I couldn't bear that.'

'But, Daisy, in this case he is responsible. Partly responsible. You didn't get pregnant on your own.'

'But he doesn't want to be a father.' She pictured the way he'd looked when he'd told her about his own family, that sunny day a million years ago in Central Park. 'He had a miserable childhood, Juno. His father was violent, abusive. But he didn't blame his dad for what he did to him and to his brother and sisters. Honestly, when he was telling me about it, reading between the lines, it was like he blamed himself. I think that's why he's so scared of making a commitment. I'm not going to force it on him. I love him, how could I?' she said, placing her hands on her belly.

Juno stood up and paced across the room. 'That is such a load of total rubbish.' She stabbed an indignant finger at her friend. 'Stop being such a martyr. It's not your fault you got pregnant.'

'I know, but I want this baby.' She caressed her stomach, felt the jolt of emotion. 'Whatever the problems, the challenges, the difficulties I'll have to face. This is like a dream come true for me.' Maybe not the whole dream, but a good part of it. 'I think it could well be Connor's worst nightmare.' And then another thought occurred to her. 'Plus, I spent my whole childhood around men that didn't want to be my dad. I know how inadequate that can make you feel. I'm not going to put my own child through that. I couldn't.'

Juno gave a deep sigh. 'Okay, fine, have it your way, Daisy. But I still think you're wrong.' She sat back on the bed. 'And if he finds out, there could be hell to pay.'

'He's not going to find out. He looked horrified after I told him I loved him. I don't think he's going to go to any great lengths to seek me out. Plus he's moving soon. All I have to do is be careful and keep a low profile.'

Juno slanted her a rueful look. 'Yes, and we all know how good you are at that,' she muttered.

CHAPTER SEVENTEEN

'I'LL kill ye little bastards.'

Connor flinched at the slurred shout, scrambled back at the angry thud on the door. The sharp crack as the thin plywood splintered had flop sweat trickling down beneath his T-shirt, stinging the welts from two nights back.

'He means it, Con. He really means it this time,' came Mac's panicked whisper.

Connor flung an arm round his brother's shoulder. 'Soon as he gets in, you go on. Get the girls to Mrs Flaherty's. I'll hold him off.'

They jumped together as another loud crack ripped the air. Connor's gaze was riveted to the tiny latch, hanging by the last two screws. Queasy fear gripped his stomach, the memory of the pain so vivid his muscles tensed, his back throbbed. The thundering in his ears cut out the crash as the door fell forward in slow, silent motion. Connor raised his arms, the thin whimper of Mac's crying piercing the mute terror as the dark shape stumbled towards them. Vicious pain sliced across his shoulder as the belt tore into tender flesh.

Connor bolted forward into darkness, his hands reaching for something that wasn't there.

His chest screamed as he struggled to breathe, his ears ringing with the sound of leather cutting flesh, his shoulders livid with the phantom pain.

He choked down a gulp of air.

Just a nightmare. Just a nightmare. Get a grip, Brody.

Gradually his eyes adjusted to the dim light, saw the plush drapes, the shadows cast by moonlight in the garden beyond. He braced his hands on the bed, let his chin drop to his chest, waited for his mind to adjust, to yank him out of the horror.

But as he waited an eternity to draw that first steady breath the silence echoed around him. The emptiness, the loneliness taunted him.

Why wasn't she here? He needed her.

As his breathing evened out at last he covered his face with his hands, pushed shaking fingers through his hair. Two whole days. Two long, miserable days. And the yearning, the desperation hadn't faded; they had only got worse.

He blew out a breath and finally accepted the truth. He'd mucked everything up.

How could he have been so stupid? What the hell had he thrown away? All this time he'd been running away from the one thing he should have been running towards.

He lifted the sheet, damp with his sweat, settled back into the bed. The residue of the nightmare rippled through him, making his muscles quake.

He shut his eyes and swore that tomorrow he'd make it right. He'd do whatever he had to do, to get Daisy back where she belonged.

'We need to talk.'

Daisy stared in shock as the very last man she'd expected to see, or wanted to see, stood in her doorway.

'Go away.' She went to slam the door.

He slapped his hand against it. 'I will not.' He shoved the door open and strode past her into the tiny bedsit.

'You can't come in here.' Outrage was closely followed by panic. She'd been sick twice already since waking up an hour ago and could feel the stirrings of a new bout of nausea in the pit of her stomach.

'Too bad. I'm in already.' He stood in the middle of the room, his broad shoulders and determined scowl making the small space look a great deal smaller.

'Please leave, Connor. Our fling's over.' She tried to keep the quiver out of her voice. She had to get him out of here, before he saw her vomit. What if he put two and two together? She'd wrestled with what she had to do for two whole days. She hadn't seen hide or hair of him and, while her heart had yearned for even a quick glimpse, she knew she'd made the right decision not to tell him about the baby.

Trust Connor to turn up unexpectedly, though, and ruin her best intentions.

'I've got nothing more to say to you,' she said. 'And this is just embarrassing us both.'

'As if I care about embarrassing,' he shouted back. 'It so happens, I've got a piece to say to you and I'm going to say it. You had your say, two days ago, when you stormed off in a huff. Now I'm having mine.'

'I don't care what you have to say…' She stopped in mid-shout, clasping her hand over her mouth, the sick waves heaving up her abdomen.

He was beside her in a second, gripping her arm. 'What's wrong? You look sick.'

'Get out!' she shouted, then shot out of the room and dashed down the hall to the bathroom.

Connor stood stock-still and listened to Daisy's feet fly down the corridor. So that was the way of it? She loved him so much, he made her retch.

He sat on the bed, dropped his head in his hands.

Damn, what was the matter with him? He was handling this all wrong. You didn't turn up on a woman's doorstep to tell her you loved her and straight off start yelling. What the hell had happened to all the easy charm he'd used on women so effortlessly in the past?

He heaved out a breath. Stood up, hopelessly restless and confused.

He'd be gentle when she got back. She was obviously poorly. Problem was, he'd never done anything like this before and had no practice whatsoever at it. Was he supposed to get down on one knee? Make an idiot of himself? Probably.

He glanced round the small, cluttered room, noticed the fanciful scene she'd painted on the ceiling and sighed.

This could well be the most important moment of his life and he'd mucked it up beautifully. He knew he had a lot of making up to do, after his knee-jerk reaction two days ago, but he didn't have an idea in his head how to do it. What did he know of romance? For sure, he'd talked women into bed before, but he'd never once had to bare his soul to one. He'd spent all morning practising what to say. But in the end he'd got so frustrated he'd come storming in here like a hurricane and blown it completely.

He paced up to her vanity, picked up the little vial of perfume, sniffed. The familiar scent filled him with the same bone-deep longing he'd had in the night, after waking up from his nightmare, and in the past two days as he'd waited like a fool for his feelings to level, to change.

He put the vial down carefully. Scowled when he saw something next to it on the edge of the sink. He picked the small plastic bottle up, squinting at the label.

'Pregnacare Vitamins,' he said aloud. 'What the…?'

'Oh, no.' He heard the pained whisper, looked round to see Daisy standing by the door, a panicked look on her face. His heart began to pound, but it wasn't panic clawing up his throat as he would have expected, but hope blossoming. Bright, beautiful, glorious hope.

He held the bottle up. 'What are these, now?'

She walked towards him, whipped the bottle out of his

hand and buried it in the pocket of her bathrobe. 'Nothing, now go away.'

She turned her back on him, her shoulders rigid with tension, and wrapped her hands around her waist.

He stepped up to her, went to touch her, but pulled his hands away. He wanted to hold her, just hold her for ever. But he knew he didn't have the right. Not yet. The lump in his throat made it hard for him to speak. 'You weren't going to tell me?'

She didn't look round, but her shoulders softened, and he heard her weary sigh. 'Please go away, Connor. Pretend you never saw those. Your life can go on as you want it. And so can mine.'

He rested his hands on her shoulders, unable to hold back any longer, and turned her to face him. She had her eyes downcast but he could see a silent tear running down her cheek. It pierced his heart. He tucked a thumb under her chin, forced her gaze to meet his. 'Is that really how you want it? Don't you trust me? Don't you trust your own feelings?'

She let out a soft sob, bit hard into her lip. 'What if I told you it's not even yours?' she said, desperation edging her voice.

'I'd know you were lying.' He brushed the tear away with his thumb. 'You're a terrible liar, Daisy, you know.' He pressed his lips to hers. 'I love you, Daisy. That's what I came to tell you. Although I've made a mess of it so far. Tell me it's not too late.'

Daisy had thought her heart couldn't feel any more pain, that she couldn't possibly cry any more tears, but hearing him say the words she had dreamed of hearing the last few days and knowing they weren't true felt like the worst pain yet. More tears welled over her lids.

'Don't, Connor. I don't believe you.'

'You're kidding.' He gave a brittle laugh, then frowned. 'I've never told a living soul I loved them before. And now when I do you don't believe me? Talk about Murphy's Law. Why don't you believe me?' He sounded annoyed and exasperated, but then his fingers touched her cheek. The tenderness, the understanding in his eyes shocked her. 'This is because of your mother, isn't it?' he said softly. 'Because she looked for love and didn't find it, you won't believe it when it's standing right here in front of you.'

She searched his face, desperate to believe him, desperate to take what he offered. He was right, her experiences as a child had made her wary of love. But as she looked at him all she could see was his frustration, and his determination.

She drew back, remembering only too well the look on his face two days ago, when she'd told him she loved him. She shook her head.

She couldn't let herself hope for the impossible. She knew the truth. She'd worked it all out, sensibly and rationally. People didn't change. They didn't. Her mother had proved that with every man she'd fallen in love with.

'I knew you'd do this,' she whispered. 'I knew you'd feel responsible. You didn't love me two days ago, and you don't love me now. You don't want to be a father and you don't want me, not really.' She held his forearms, tried to push him away, but he wouldn't let her go. 'I knew if I told you about the baby you'd want to do the right thing. Just like you did for your brother and your sisters. You took a belt for them, Connor. You let him beat you rather than see them get hurt, didn't you? But I'm not going to be another belt. Because that's what I'd be if I let you do the thing that was right for me and not for you.'

He dragged her closer, rested his forehead on hers.

'Daisy, that's so sweet.' He lifted his head and sent her a tentative smile that made her insides feel all shaky. 'But it's also total rubbish. I want you. I need you. I love you. And I loved you two days ago but I was too stupid to see it. And I'm over the moon that by some miracle I got you pregnant.' He cocked his head, the smile widening. 'Although we'll have to have a little talk about how that happened. Because for the life of me I'm sure I used condoms the whole time.' He was grinning at her now. 'And if I can get you pregnant through bonded latex we may have to be a lot more careful if we don't want to end up with twenty kids. But first things first. How am I going to get it into that thick head of yours that I love you?'

She pushed away from him, her anger rising. Why was he making this so hard? 'All right then, tell me why you reacted the way you did two days ago. When I told you I loved you, you looked absolutely horrified.'

Connor swore softly and felt the joy, the hope fade.

So it was all going to boil down to this. He'd have to tell her his darkest shame and hope against hope that she could still love him afterwards. 'Are you sure you want to know this?'

Her lips firmed into a grim line of determination. She nodded.

He let her go, sat on her bed. He'd hurt her, when he hadn't meant to; now he could destroy everything—but it was a risk he'd have to take.

'If I tell you, you might change your mind about loving me,' he said, hoping to give her a get-out clause.

She didn't take it. 'No, I won't,' she said with complete certainty.

He took a deep breath, but he couldn't look at her and tell her, so he gazed down at his hands, fisted in his lap. 'You're right. I took the belt if I could. Mac and me both. But I wasn't being brave, or noble particularly. It was just, they were so little, my sisters, and they loved me. And Mac, he looked up to me, thought I knew all the answers. They all depended on me to keep them safe, to keep us together.' He shrugged, shame thickening his voice. 'But one night, I sneaked out. Maeve Gallagher had promised me heaven the last time I'd seen her. I'd fresh scars from his last drinking session and he'd come home and fallen straight into his bed. I thought they'd be safe, that no harm would come to them. I swear it.'

She sat beside him, put her hand over his. But he still couldn't look at her, couldn't bear to see her contempt at what he'd done. 'But when I got home, there was a commotion outside. The neighbours were crowded about the house. There were lights flashing.' He could still picture it all so clearly even now, hear the murmur of curious voices, smell the scent of peat fires and winter frost and feel the chilling fear that had had him scrambling head first through the crowd. 'The Garda had my Da, he had his head bent, his hands cuffed behind his back. And then I saw the ambulance and Mac.' He gulped down air, tried to steady himself. 'He was lying on a stretcher. He looked so small, his face battered, his arm all crooked. I thought he was dead.' He forced himself to meet her eyes. 'He wasn't dead, but I never saw him again. Him or the girls. I told the social worker I didn't want to. But the truth is I couldn't bear to face them.'

'Why couldn't you?' she asked, her love clear on her face despite all that he'd told her. It gave him the courage he needed to tell her the last of it.

'Because I'd let them down. It was my job to protect them and I'd failed. I didn't deserve to be their brother, not any more.'

Daisy cupped Connor's face in her palms. Seeing the pain in his eyes, the regret, the guilt, she realised she loved this man more than life itself. She tried to speak, but emotion closed her throat.

He gripped her wrists, drew her hands down. 'When you told me you loved me,' he said, 'I was so scared. Scared to love you back. Because after that night, I promised I'd never love a living soul again and risk letting them get hurt. Risk losing them.'

'Connor, it wasn't your fault,' she whispered, the tears flowing freely down her cheeks. 'You were a boy trying to do something even a grown man couldn't do. You didn't let them down. And as long as you love me as much as I love you, you could never let me down either.'

He threaded his fingers through hers, held on. 'I do love you. More than you know. But are you sure that's enough?' he asked.

She pressed her palm to his cheek. 'Of course it is. You silly idiot.'

He blew out a breath, the relief plain on his face as he lent into her palm. 'That's a fine thing to call the man that loves you and is the father of your baby,' he said, emotion deepening his voice.

She smiled, for what felt like the first time in a millennium, and threw her arms round his neck. She clung onto him so tightly she wasn't sure he could breathe.

He chuckled. 'So does this mean you believe I love you now?' he said, his voice muffled against her hair.

She nodded, the joy coursing through her making it hard for her to breathe too.

His arms banded round her waist. 'And there'll be no more doubting it?'

She nodded again, even more vigorously, then whispered, 'I'd like my engagement ring back, now. Please.'

His breath tickled her ear lobe as he laughed. 'I'll think on it,' he said, but she could hear the teasing note in his voice. He lifted his head, framed her face in warm palms, his eyes shining with love. How could she ever have doubted him?

'But first I need you to do something for me,' he murmured.

'What's that?' she asked.

His thumb caressed the pulse in her throat as his hands settled on her shoulders. 'Come home,' he said as his gaze remained locked on hers. 'Come home with me where you belong.'

She thrust her fingers into his hair, brought his lips to hers and gave him his answer in a kiss bursting with love, heat, hope and commitment—and pure, unadulterated joy.

EPILOGUE

'FOR goodness' sake, let me look, you meanie. I've waited weeks already,' Daisy ordered, her fingers grappling with the immovable hands covering her eyes.

'Hold your horses now.' Connor's deep chuckle next to her ear sounded both amused and a bit too smug for her liking. 'I'll let you loose when I'm good and ready and not a moment before. Juno, get the lights,' he shouted past her as his chest pressed into her back. 'There now. What do you make of it?'

His hands lifted and Daisy blinked, the dazzle of fluorescent light blinding her. As the sleek, beautiful lines of glass and wood came into focus through the smell of fresh paint and sawdust she gasped. She slapped her hands over her mouth as tears welled in her eyes and emotion clogged her throat. 'Oh,' was the only word she could utter.

'That bad, eh?' Connor said beside her, sounding a lot less smug.

She turned, bounced up on her toes and flung her hands round his shoulders, nearly knocking him over with her belly in the process. 'Oh, my God, Connor. It's exactly the way I envisioned it. Exactly what I wanted. How did you do it? And how did you do it so fast?'

He'd given her another of her dreams, she thought, her heart bursting with love and excitement. And this was one she hadn't even realised she'd wanted. In fact she'd needed quite a lot of persuading to start with.

Six months ago when he'd walked into the bathroom after she'd just finished puking and informed her he'd bought her a shop at auction that morning, she'd had the distinct urge to throttle him, if she recalled correctly.

Was he insane? Why hadn't he discussed it with her first? He might enjoy being impulsive, reckless even, but she didn't. How was she going to organise refurbishing a shop? Then manage it and supply it while she was suffering from the worst case of morning sickness known to woman? And how would she handle all the extra responsibility when the baby was born?

But over the months her doubts had faded along with the morning sickness, and the excitement of having her own proper space to display her designs, her own workshop in the back to manufacture them, had built to impossible proportions.

And through it all Connor had been there, by her side. Encouraging her ideas, offering suggestions about the refurbishment, organising the construction, insisting she hire a manager so she could devote her time to designing, overseeing his crew with calm efficiency through all the inevitable hiccups—and on one memorable evening strapping on his tool belt to put up the shelving in the workshop and then letting her seduce him in the newly installed bathroom afterwards.

The experience had brought them even closer together. They weren't just a couple any more, they were a unit, with a shared dream.

In the last month though, with her approaching the end of her pregnancy he'd insisted she stay at home as he and the crew installed the cabinets and counters, finished the fitting rooms and did all the painting and decorating. And she had to admit she'd been a little miffed by his high-handedness. But she still couldn't believe how he had transformed that empty shell from four short weeks ago into the dream come true she saw before her now.

'I didn't do it on my own,' he said, smiling down at her.

'Oh, I know, you must thank all the crew. Are we going to have a proper opening, with champagne? We'll have to invite them all. I was thinking we could have it in a month if we get our skates on and—'

'We'll be doing no such thing,' he said firmly, interrupting her excited babble. He slung his arm round her shoulder and drew her close. 'The grand opening will have to wait a while.' He stroked his palm across her huge belly and she felt the heat right down to her toes. 'You're going to be busy for the next little while, looking after yourself and my child. This place is to be off limits until Junior's out and you're up and about. We'll schedule the opening for July, but only if you behave.'

'But that's ridiculous, that's months away,' she sputtered, starting to feel a little miffed again.

'And Juno here is under strict instructions to make sure you do as you're told.' He winked at Juno. 'Is that right, Juno?'

'Aye aye, Connor.' Juno gave a mock salute, grinning at Connor. The sight warmed Daisy's heart, despite her frustration with the two of them. How could it not?

Connor had gone out of his way to win Juno over since Daisy and he had started living together. It hadn't been easy at first, Juno's hostility towards him making her prickly and tense. But he'd worn her down over time, first getting her to accept him, then getting her to let go of her suspicion of good-looking men, at least as far as he was concerned, and finally engineering an easy friendship between them that had sprung from their mutual love for Daisy.

He treated Juno like a little sister, advising her and looking out for her and teasing her, while she treated him like an older brother, only taking the advice she felt she needed, and teasing him mercilessly right back.

But right now, as Daisy watched the silent communication between them, she was beginning to wonder if they weren't like brother and sister after all. But more like evil twins.

She could feel herself pouting. She hated being ganged up on. 'The baby's not due for two whole weeks.' She scowled at them both. 'Surely I can get a bit done in here before then.' She waddled over to the beautifully carved walnut counter tops, ran her palm lovingly across the smooth, vanished wood. 'We can't just leave it sitting here empty all that time.'

Connor stepped up behind her, wrapped his arms round her enormous waist and hugged her close. 'We can and we will,' he murmured, his breath feathering her ear. 'And from the size of you I'd say two weeks is optimistic, angel.'

She stuck an elbow in his ribs. 'Thanks a bunch. I know I look like a barrage balloon but you don't have to keep reminding me.'

'Stop fishing for compliments.' He chuckled. 'You know right well you're gorgeous.'

Daisy felt herself softening at the compliment. The man's charm was deadly.

He placed his hand over hers on the wood, brought her fingers to his lips. 'There's no rush, Daisy. We've all the time in the world, you know.'

Daisy gave a resigned sigh, the huge rush of love making her chest ache, and knew he'd got her, again. Then she heard a loud choking sound from behind them.

'If you two are going to get all drippy, I'm off,' Juno said, her voice light.

The deep rumble of Connor's laugh reverberated against Daisy's back. 'You best go, then, because drippy's definitely on the cards right enough.'

'You don't have to ask me twice,' Juno shot back, sounding more carefree than Daisy had ever known her. 'I'll be round tomorrow, Daze,' she called across to her. 'To stand guard.'

Daisy leaned round Connor. 'You traitor,' she said and grinned.

'Absolutely.' Juno gave a jaunty wave and left, slamming the shop door behind her.

'Right.' Connor pulled her back into his embrace. 'Now

little Juno the killjoy's out the way and I've got you all to myself, there's one other thing we need to talk about. And I want this settled before the baby's born. So you can cut out the delaying tactics.'

'What's that now?' Daisy said in her best Irish brogue, although she had a pretty good idea what he was referring to. After all he'd been banging on about it for months.

'You know full well what. We've yet to set the wedding date.'

'I told you, I don't want to get married looking like a beached whale.'

'And, while you look nothing like a beached whale,' he said, sounding pained, 'I agreed to that bit of fancy, didn't I? You've a few months once Junior's born to get yourself together, but then we're doing it. I found a place in France that would be perfect. It's available for the third Saturday in August. We can party there with all our pals for a week and be back in time for Carnival. I've a mind to book it tomorrow. What do you say?'

She wanted to say yes, there was nothing more she wanted to do than marry this man and claim him as her own for everyone to see. But something had been bothering her for months about their wedding. Something that had nothing to do with her figure. And she still hadn't found the best way to broach the subject.

'I thought you said we had all the time in the world,' she said lamely.

He huffed and turned her in his arms. Keeping his hands on her hips, he dipped his head to look into her face. 'Is there another reason you won't set the date? Because if there is you best spit it out now.'

She swallowed hard, could see the stubbornness in the hard line of his jaw and knew this was it. She would have to say it now, or for ever hold her peace. And that she couldn't do. Connor needed closure on the horrors of his childhood, and he would never have it unless he took this next step.

She took a deep breath. 'I want to contact Mac,' she blurted out. 'I want to invite him to the wedding.'

His eyebrows shot up. 'You… What?'

'He's your brother, Connor. We're having a baby in a few weeks and he'll be its uncle. And when we get married we'll be saying vows that will make us a family for ever. I want him there to witness them with us. Don't you?'

His hands fell from her waist. He looked shocked. But at least he didn't look angry or defensive, which were the two reactions she'd feared the most.

'What…?' His voice broke. He cleared his throat. 'What if he won't come?'

She took his hands in hers, squeezed. 'If he's your brother, he can't possibly be that much of a coward.' She was counting on it. 'You need to forgive yourself for what happened that night—and to do that you need to see Mac again, to make things right with him. He's your family which makes him my family too.' She paused, willing him to understand. 'If you don't want to contact him, I'll accept your decision and we'll never talk about it again. But I had to ask.'

He sucked in a long breath, raised his eyes to the ceiling, and slowly let it out. 'You are the most contrary woman…' he muttered, but there was no heat in the words.

His eyes met hers. 'Okay, you go ahead and contact Mac. But I hope he's ready for what's about to hit him.'

She wrapped her arms around his neck and smacked a kiss on his lips. 'Thank you, Connor. It's the right thing to do, I know it is. And if everything goes well with Mac, we could start trying to trace your sis—'

He slapped his hand over her mouth before she could say another word. 'Stop right there. There'll be no more meddling until we're married, the shop's up and running and the baby's at least five. Do you understand?'

She nodded behind his hand, her heart swelling at the rueful grin on his face. He wasn't mad. He didn't seem upset. He might even be a little pleased about the plan to contact his brother. Everything was going to work out, she was sure of it.

'Now, when I lift my hand,' he said carefully, the mischievous twinkle in his eyes belying the severity in his voice, 'I want you to say you'll make an honest man of me on August eighteenth. No more excuses. You got it?'

She nodded. He lifted his hand.

'Aye, aye, Connor,' she chirped, feeling as if all the happiness in the world had just exploded in her heart.

'And none of your cheek either,' he said, then took her in his arms and kissed her into complete submission to seal the deal.

Three days and fourteen excruciating hours of labour later, and Daisy held another of her dreams in tired arms. As little Ronan Cormac Brody suckled ferociously at her breast, and his father stared down at the two of them, his arm tight around Daisy's shoulders and his eyes filled with awe, Daisy knew she had the happy ever after she'd once only dreamed of in some secret corner of her heart.

Now all she had to do was start living it.

* * * * *

A LIGHT, INQUIRING KNOCK SOUNDED on the door, and, turning from that grim reminder, Aarif left the bathroom and went to fulfill his brother's bidding, and express his greetings to his bride.

The official led him to the double doors of the Throne Room; inside, an expectant hush fell like a curtain being dropped into place, or perhaps pulled up.

"Your Eminence," the official said in French, the national language of Zaraq, his voice low and unctuous, "may I present His Royal Highness, King Zakari."

Aarif choked; the sound was lost amid a ripple of murmurings from the palace staff, who had assembled for this honored occasion. It would take King Bahir only one glance to realize it was not the king who graced his Throne Room today, but rather the king's brother, a lowly prince.

Aarif felt a flash of rage—directed at himself. A mistake had been made in the correspondence, he supposed. He'd delegated the task to an aide when he should have written himself and explained that he would be coming rather than his brother.

Now he would have to explain the mishap in front of company—all of Bahir's staff—and he feared the insult could be great.

"Your Eminence," he said, also speaking French, and

moved into the long, narrow room with its frescoed ceilings and bare walls. He bowed, not out of obeisance but rather respect, and heard Bahir shift in his chair. "I fear my brother, His Royal Highness Zakari, was unable to attend to this glad errand, due to pressing royal business. I am honored to escort his bride, the princess Kalila, to Calista in his stead."

Bahir was silent, and, stifling a prickle of both alarm and irritation, Aarif rose. He was conscious of Bahir watching him, his skin smooth but his eyes shrewd, his mouth tightening with disappointment or displeasure, perhaps both.

Yet even before Bahir made a reply, even before the formalities had been dispensed with, Aarif found his gaze sliding, of its own accord, to the silent figure to Bahir's right.

It was his daughter, of course. Kalila. Aarif had a memory of a pretty, precocious child. He'd spoken a few words to her at the engagement party more than ten years ago now. Yet now the woman standing before him was lovely, although, he acknowledged wryly, he could see little of her.

Her head was bowed, her figure swathed in a kaftan, and yet, as if she felt the magnetic tug of his gaze, she lifted her head and her eyes met his.

It was all he could see of her, those eyes; they were almond-shaped, wide and dark, luxuriously fringed, a deep, clear golden brown. Every emotion could be seen in them, including the one that flickered there now as her gaze was drawn inexorably to his face, to his scar.

It was disgust Aarif thought he saw flare in their golden depths, and as their gazes held and clashed he felt a sharp, answering stab of disappointment and self-loathing in his own gut.

* * * * *

Be sure to look for
THE SHEIKH'S FORBIDDEN VIRGIN
by Kate Hewitt,
available October from Harlequin Presents®!

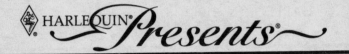

TWO CROWNS, TWO ISLANDS, ONE LEGACY

A royal family torn apart by pride and its lust for power, reunited by purity and passion

THE ROYAL HOUSE
of
KAREDES

Look for the next passionate adventure in
The Royal House of Karedes:

THE SHEIKH'S FORBIDDEN VIRGIN
by Kate Hewitt, October 2009

THE GREEK BILLIONAIRE'S INNOCENT PRINCESS
by Chantelle Shaw, November 2009

THE FUTURE KING'S LOVE-CHILD
by Melanie Milburne, December 2009

RUTHLESS BOSS, ROYAL MISTRESS
by Natalie Anderson, January 2010

THE DESERT KING'S HOUSEKEEPER BRIDE
by Carol Marinelli, February 2010

REQUEST YOUR FREE BOOKS!

HARLEQUIN *Presents*®

2 FREE NOVELS PLUS 2 FREE GIFTS!

PASSION GUARANTEED SEDUCTION

YES! Please send me 2 FREE Harlequin Presents® novels and my 2 FREE gifts (gifts are worth about $10). After receiving them, if I don't wish to receive any more books, I can return the shipping statement marked "cancel". If I don't cancel, I will receive 6 brand-new novels every month and be billed just $4.05 per book in the U.S. or $4.74 per book in Canada. That's a savings of close to 15% off the cover price! It's quite a bargain! Shipping and handling is just 50¢ per book*. I understand that accepting the 2 free books and gifts places me under no obligation to buy anything. I can always return a shipment and cancel at any time. Even if I never buy another book, the two free books and gifts are mine to keep forever.   106 HDN EYRQ 306 HDN EYR2

Name	(PLEASE PRINT)	

Address		Apt. #

City	State/Prov.	Zip/Postal Code

Signature (if under 18, a parent or guardian must sign)

Mail to the **Harlequin Reader Service:**
IN U.S.A.: P.O. Box 1867, Buffalo, NY 14240-1867
IN CANADA: P.O. Box 609, Fort Erie, Ontario L2A 5X3

Not valid to current subscribers of Harlequin Presents books.

Are you a current subscriber of Harlequin Presents books and want to receive the larger-print edition? Call 1-800-873-8635 today!

* Terms and prices subject to change without notice. Prices do not include applicable taxes. Sales tax applicable in N.Y. Canadian residents will be charged applicable provincial taxes and GST. Offer not valid in Quebec. This offer is limited to one order per household. All orders subject to approval. Credit or debit balances in a customer's account(s) may be offset by any other outstanding balance owed by or to the customer. Please allow 4 to 6 weeks for delivery. Offer available while quantities last.

Your Privacy: Harlequin Books is committed to protecting your privacy. Our Privacy Policy is available online at www.eHarlequin.com or upon request from the Reader Service. From time to time we make our lists of customers available to reputable third parties who may have a product or service of interest to you. If you would prefer we not share your name and address, please check here. ☐

HP09R

You're invited to join our Tell Harlequin Reader Panel!

By joining our new reader panel you will:

- Receive Harlequin® books—they are FREE and yours to keep with no obligation to purchase anything!
- Participate in fun online surveys
- Exchange opinions and ideas with women just like you
- Have a say in our new book ideas and help us publish the best in women's fiction

In addition, you will have a chance to win great prizes and receive special gifts! See Web site for details. Some conditions apply. Space is limited.

To join, visit us at
www.TellHarlequin.com.

I ♥

HARLEQUIN *Presents*
